KILLER FLIES

Mark Kendall

For the gamers
(you know who you are)
who taught me how to adventure

Encyclopocalypse Publications
www.encyclopocalypse.com

Contents

Prologue   5

Chapter One   7

Chapter Two   15

Chapter Three   23

Chapter Four   31

Chapter Five   45

Chapter Six   55

Chapter Seven   65

Chapter Eight   77

Chapter Nine   87

Chapter Ten   95

Chapter Eleven   105

Chapter Twelve   115

Chapter Thirteen   123

Chapter Fourteen   135

Chapter Fifteen   145

Chapter Sixteen   151

Chapter Seventeen   159

Chapter Eighteen   171

Chapter Nineteen   177

About the Author   183

Prologue

"Shit!" Josh Gatlin flicked the broken match out the window of the covered truck. Before him the sky was darkening as the sun dropped behind the peaks surrounding the speeding truck. It was just like old Sánchez to send him to Albuquerque, over eighty miles to the south, at twenty-to-five. Irritably he struck a second match and lit the cigarette hanging precariously from his lower lip.

What could be so fucking important that a guy had to make a two-hour drive at quitting time? He hadn't even had a chance to call Juanita and tell her that he'd be late. Well, they'd just have to miss that movie, but there were other ways to pass an evening. His mouth grew dry as he thought of her soft brown thighs slowly opening to him.

His attention wandered from the steep curving mountain road with its deep canyon to one side as he thought of the lovely Chicana. He'd gone with some friends one night to the Senate Bar to do a little Mex baiting, but instead of fighting he'd become a lover. Juanita had been waiting table that night, and the way her black eyes had dared him to insult her had caught him. He'd gone back at closing time, hanging around on the sidewalk until she'd come out. Man, the sparks had flown when she'd seen him, but she let him walk her home and then there was no way he was leaving.

He pulled his left hand from the wheel and wiped at the beads of sweat forming on his upper lip. Yeah, he thought, I'll call her on my way through Santa Fe.

Maybe she can even ride along with me. Now that'd be a trip worth making.

Out of the shadows the shambling red form lurched onto the highway. Frantically Gatlin spun the wheel, but it was too late. The truck plowed into the cow. The animal gave a scream of anguish as metal crumpled and blood spurted across the windshield.

The truck keeled over, landing with a shriek of outraged metal on its side. Over the ripped tailgate tumbled the boxes. They fell gracefully down the cliff face, breaking open as the rocks rose up to meet them, and releasing their seething, buzzing cargo.

Gatlin struggled to pull himself up on the twisted door of the truck, but he collapsed, screaming, as his shattered leg buckled beneath him. Panting, he lay on the rough gravel along the side of the road. Dazed, and bemused from the pain, he watched hypnotized as the black mass settled onto the carcass of the cow. After what seemed hours, but was in reality only minutes, the strange writhing ballet ceased. The seething, undulating mass spiraled upward from the bloody hulk that had once been a living creature.

Bile rose with the scream in his throat as Gatlin was enfolded by the buzzing black shadow.

Chapter One

The tip of a small pink tongue peeked from between the lips of the brown-haired child as she carefully colored in the dancer's skirt. The afternoon sun, slanting through the windows of the rambling adobe house, gleamed on the polished brick floor of the kitchen.

The skirt completed to her satisfaction, she slipped the blue Crayola back into the box before her and in a dilatory fashion studied the rainbow of colors.

The oppressive heat of the July afternoon had managed to penetrate even the two-foot-thick mud Walls of the house, and with a weary sigh the child scrubbed at her damp matted bangs. She glanced at the frying pan shaped clock on the wall and sighed.

"Three o'clock," she stated aloud. It was nice to hear a voice even if it was only her own. "I wonder when Momma and Hutch are gonna be home," she asked the brown mongrel who lay beneath her chair. The dog's tail thumped in answer.

She really should have gone to Mountainedge, she decided. But it had sounded so fun and grown-up to stay home alone and be in charge of the ranch.

Absently she peeled the paper from a Crayola. If she'd gone with them, Momma would probably have bought her a soda at Keller's Drugstore. She wished they would bring home ice cream, but with a sigh realized that it would never last through the forty-mile drive in this heat.

"Well, maybe she got the cookies with the marshmallow inside," she confided to her pet. One sleepy brown eye regarded her, then drooped shut once more.

"Skeets," she said, exasperated, "You're not listening to me!" The tail thumped again.

Selecting another crayon, she returned *to* her coloring book. A small whimper drew her attention. Skeets stood with his paws on the windowsill gazing nervously outside. She slid from the chair; the sound of her cowboy boots on the brick floor was very loud in the silence. Hesitantly she joined the dog.

That was what had made Skeets cry, she decided. It was *so* quiet. The cattle in the bottom field weren't lowing and even the birds had fallen silent. Anxiously she hugged the soft furry body next to her.

A piercing buzz cut through the air. With a yelp the dog leaped from the room, its tail tucked firmly between its legs.

"Skeets," she called, racing after him, but she froze at the door into the living room as a terrified scream ripped through the buzzing. An animal in terror, more particularly a horse, and the girl knew that the only horse near the house was Rosebud... *her* Rosebud.

The shrill screams gave way to gut-wrenching moans. Grabbing the shotgun from its position by the back door, the child flew down the steps and into the dusty yard.

A small white pony, its coat now almost black beneath a layer of writhing insects, staggered hysterically about the corral. Blood streamed from the tender skin around its eyes and muzzle, and the groaning snorts broke the child's control.

With a scream she charged to the wood fence and scrambled over. Using the gun like a club, she beat at the flies that sucked greedily at her horse. With a final groan the pony fell to its knees and rolled onto its side.

Tears streamed down the child's reddened face. "Rosebud! Rosebud! Don't be dead, you can't be dead!" The last word was shrieked, for the flies had sensed fresher blood, a prey yet living.

In a matter of minutes they were gone. The heat-dreaming silence had returned. The only sound was that of a dog piteously whining as it licked at what had once been a human face.

"It's another scorcher today, folks!" announced the disc jockey gleefully from the comfort of his air-conditioned booth. "A hundred and two in the mountain Southwest. Stay tuned now for more great country favorites," A nasal female vocalist crooned about being lonely in a singles bar.

Sherry Quinn tossed back her long blond hair and irritably snapped off the truck's radio.

"It's bad enough that we have to live through this heat," she complained bitterly, "without them telling us every fifteen minutes how hot it is."

Her companion laughed, deepening the creases about his gray eyes. His teeth gleamed white against his sun-bronzed skin. "Come on, honey," drawled Hutch Engels. "Rainy season's comin'. It's gonna break soon."

"I just hope I don't break first," the woman retorted. Glancing out the rear window, she watched the dust stream away behind the speeding wheels of the pickup. Dust coated the pines lining the road and a thin film of the fine grit lay across the windshield. Leaning against the door, she stole a glance at Engels. His eyes were on the dirt road ahead, and he thoughtfully flicked a toothpick from one side of his mouth to the other. The hot breeze blowing through the open window tugged at his sun-bleached hair.

She wondered how she could have been so numb after Tom's death not to notice how handsome Hutch was. All through those terrible first months he'd been there, quiet and steady. And if he hadn't stayed, she'd have had to sell the ranch and return with Pammy to her folks' home in Illinois.

"Why did you stay?" she asked suddenly, still watching him.

"Because you needed me," he replied simply, his eyes never straying from the rutted track before him.

"You could have gone back to the rodeo circuit. Lot more money there than I could offer you."

"After that last old bull tore me up, and when Tom gave me a job even though I looked like a walkin' jigsaw puzzle, I knew I didn't want to go back to rodeo." He cocked an affectionate eye toward her. "Besides, I was raised to be a real cowboy, not a fancy bronc rider. My daddy never could abide rodeo, said it was a waste of good men and fine animals."

"Then why did you do it?"

"After we lost the ranch I was in no mood to work for somebody else."

"Then why on earth did you stick with us?" she asked again, exasperated.

"You're special," he replied laconically.

"I'm glad, Hutch," she murmured softly. His hand, rough and callused, captured hers where it rested on the seat of the truck. She made no move, just sat comfortably enjoying the contact.

"I'm gonna start cutting that back pasture tomorrow. The rain should hold off until the grass has dried," he said.

"Fine. If we get as nice a cutting as May's we should be set for winter." His thumb had begun to trace a lazy circle on the palm of her hand, and Sherry found her thoughts straying from hay. The trickle of sweat running down between her shoulder blades wasn't due totally to the heat of the day.

"Pammy should have come with us," said Sherry

suddenly, forcing her thoughts from the sensual touch.

"Yeah, I thought of her all the way to the bottom of that soda."

"Don't tell her, for heaven's sake," said the woman, laughing. "We'll never hear the end of it."

"I already thought of that." He fished in his shirt pocket for several seconds, then pulled out a bulging white sack.

"What have you done?"

"Take a look." He tossed the bag onto her lap.

She glanced inside, then set it aside, laughing. "She'll be sick for a week with all that."

"I wanted to get her the chocolate, but I knew it'd be soup by the time we got home. 'Sides, she loves that red licorice."

"Hutch, you're a dear."

He smiled quietly, not responding, but his hand crept over and again took possession others.

The miles rattled away beneath the wheels of the truck. The sun was beginning to drop behind the mountains, and Sherry wondered what she could bear to cook and what Pammy and Hutch would have any appetite for in the heat. She stared drowsily out the window. The sky was an intense robin's-egg blue and there wasn't even a sign of the thunderheads that usually gathered on summer afternoons. They jounced past the body of a dog lying alongside the road. The carcass was bloated from the sun and crawling with flies. Unconsciously, Sherry shivered, grasping Hutch's hand tighter.

They pulled up under one of the massive old pine trees surrounding the house, and Hutch switched off the motor. Silence hung like a pall over the house and yard. A gnawing nameless fear grew inside her, and Sherry leaped from the truck. The slamming of the door echoed through the valley. The sound seemed to remove the paralysis that gripped her throat.

"Pammy! Pammy, where are you?" The silence mocked her.

"I don't like this," said Hutch slowly, squinting in the late-afternoon sunlight. "Skeets at least should have been out to meet us."

Sherry bolted for the house.

"Wait!" The command whipped across the yard, holding her in place. Engels climbed back into the truck and pulled down the shotgun from the rack on the back window. Cocking it, he joined Sherry.

The heavy carved oak door swung easily open beneath her touch. The plant-filled entry-hall stretched before her.

"Pammy?" she whispered. Hutch pushed past her into the living room. Nothing, Pammy's new dress hung over the chair waiting to be hemmed. Her saddle sat upended against one wall.

"She's not out riding, then." His boot heels beat out a tattoo on the brick floor as he walked into the kitchen.

"Oh, my God," moaned Sherry. She rushed to the kitchen table and clutched the open coloring book to her breast. Crayons spattered onto the floor at her feet. Flinging the book back onto the table, she hurried after the ranch-hand.

Hutch turned suddenly, blocking her at the back door. "I think you ought to wait here."

"And I think you're crazy!" Her voice cracked with strain. "This is *my* child we're talking about."

Her breasts beneath the thin material of her blouse rose and fell with fear and anger.

"Sherry, look, honey-" he began, but she shouldered him anxiously aside and ran onto the back porch.

Shading her eyes with one tanned hand, she scanned the field. She thought she could see something down in the corral, but it danced and wavered in the heat and she was unable to identify it. She ran for the enclosure. Behind her she could hear Hutch following.

The dog espied her first. His piteous howls ripped through the air, and crawling to her, he licked her boots. Sherry absently stroked his head, and his howls subsided into whimpers.

She forced herself to move forward. Step by reluctant step. Her mind, yammering for escape, forced her to look first at the pony. Oozing sockets gazed up at her. The animal's mouth was open as if it still screamed for release from the horror that had killed it. The woman choked down a sob. Then she looked beyond the pony.

A single scream was torn from her throat. Then silently she knelt in the dirt and pulled the tiny, bloody form into her arms.

The man leaned, sickened and devastated, on the rifle. Hutch Engels hadn't cried since the day thirty years ago when his daddy had lost his life to a crazed bronco. But now as he stared at the slender blue-jeaned figure helplessly rocking the dead child in her arms, he feared that the tears would come.

Minutes later he gently disengaged her clutching hands from the limp form. Blood streaked the white cotton shirt, and her blue eyes were dark with shock and horror.

"Come on, baby," he murmured huskily. He began to propel her toward the house.

She balked, turning to face him. "I've got to take her inside," she said simply. "It's hot out here."

Hutch pulled her into his arms, pressing his lips to her silky hair. "Sherry, she's dead." The simple statement released the floodgate of her grief and horror. She clung to him, sobbing, as the sun fell behind the jutting peaks and night's shadows entered. Then it was over. She stepped back from him, her face ravaged, but controlled.

"You gonna be okay now?"

"Let's call the sheriff." Her voice was flat and cold with hate. "I want answers, and I want them now! Nothing kills my child. I'll find them if it takes the rest of my life!"

Chapter Two

All hospitals smell the same, Hutch thought, rubbing at his gritty eyes with the heels of his hands. He watched a nurse swaying down the hall, and for a moment he allowed the sweet rhythm of her hips to comfort him. She vanished around a corner, and with a ragged sigh he picked up his cup of coffee.

The hours since the discovery of Pammy's maimed body had been a nightmare. Sheriff Emilio Garcia had arrived, and after photographing the scene, he and his deputy had carried the child, now covered with a blanket, away in their car. Hutch and Sherry had followed, saying nothing during the long drive down to Santa Fe. And now they waited.

For three hours they'd sat in the waiting room of St. Francis' Hospital while an autopsy was performed. Hutch glanced at the clock over the nurses' station. Three-thirty A.M. Christ, he was tired. His eyes were drawn to the still figure by the window, and he felt a surge of pity and guilt. If he were tired, he could imagine how Sherry felt.

He crossed to the woman and slipped an arm around her shoulders. Her slender form sagged against him for an instant, then she pulled herself firmly upright.

"You want some coffee?"

"No."

"Something to eat?" She shook her head. "Look, honey, it's not gonna do anyone any good if you collapse."

"Hutch, please, don't push..." Her voice trailed away. He turned to follow her gaze.

Rolling down the hall came State Police Captain Ray Padilla. His brown moon of a face was shiny with sweat, and his pudgy hands folded and crimped the soft cowboy hat he always wore.

Sherry rushed to the fat man, Hutch following quietly. "'Where are the doctors?" she demanded, her eyes searching the hall. "I want to know what they found."

"Just relax, Mrs. Quinn," he said in a heavily accented voice. "It's late; the doctors were tired and I sent them home."

"You did what?" she cried.

"I can tell you anything they could, so don't get ugly with me." The traditional Chicano dislike of a determined and powerful woman was apparent in his tone.

"All right, then tell me," she ordered.

Padilla cleared his throat, his flat black eyes shifting from the window to the clock, to Hutch, anywhere but the woman before him. "It was an animal attack," he said at last. "Probably wild dogs."

"That's crazy!" Hutch said loudly.

"Hey, keep it down! You're gonna disturb the patients."

"Damn the patients," Hutch said, stepping toward Padilla. "She wasn't attacked by wild dogs. I held Pammy. Those weren't bites. There wasn't a tooth mark on her."

Padilla backed away as the big man advanced on him.

"And her clo-" Sherry's voice broke and she rubbed at her eyes. She angrily shook her head, regaining control. "Her clothes. They weren't torn. It was almost as if something had... crawled inside them and killed her." She whirled and strode back to the window.

As he stared at her rigid back, Hutch felt the impotent fury that had gripped him for hours begin to rise. He turned and jabbed his lean forefinger into the fleshy roll above Padilla's elaborate silver and turquoise belt buckle.

"Look *Mr.* Padilla, I'm gonna say this once, slowly, clearly, so you pay attention." He leaned over the smaller man, thrusting his face near Padilla's. "Pammy didn't die from no dog bites, so I want the name and number of the medical examiner."

"You can go to hell, Engels!" Padilla said belligerently. "And if you don't stop threatening a police officer-"

"You're gonna do what?" Hutch asked sarcastically. Sherry clenched her fists, feeling her nails bite into the tender skin of her palms. Inwardly she screamed for rest, for escape from the hideous scene in that corral, but her mind refused to give her the release she craved. And now these men were playing out their little macho games while her child was *dead.* Gone. She could never hold Pammy again, stroke her brown hair, have her daughter's arms around her neck.

"Oh, this is ridiculous!" Sherry said. "All I have to do is wait till eight this morning, call the county, and get the name of the examiner. I'm going to hear the truth, Captain, no matter how you may try to hide it. Come on, Hutch." She stalked toward the elevators.

"Mrs. Quinn." She paused, turning back to face Padilla. "I'm advising you not to do that. As an officer of the law-"

"Captain," she said softly, "stuff it."

"What time is it?"

He checked his watch. "Seven."

"One more hour." She stared into the milky-white depths of her margarita. Behind the couple an old drunk snored loudly in a red-leather booth of the Fiesta Bar. As Hutch watched, a fly executed a lazy loop and landed casually in the old man's toothless mouth. Hutch glanced back at Sherry. Dark smudges beneath her eyes accentuated the cut of her high cheekbones and the rich ivory of her skin. He reached out and, taking the glass from her, gripped both her hands. "She was all I had left," she said almost inaudibly. "I know."

"I always thought she looked a lot more like Tom than like me. I was glad, too. He had a lot of strength in his face. I didn't want her to look like a cheerleader."

"Is that how you see yourself?" Hutch asked, amused. "Hmm. Hutch," she said suddenly, "I can't stand it anymore. Let's get out of here."

Slapping money onto the table, he followed her into the narrow cobblestoned street. The sun had thrust above the Sangre de Cristo Mountains, painting the adobe buildings of the historic capital gold. The minutes ticked away with their steps as they walked silent and driven through the narrow, winding streets of the city.

They found a secluded pay phone in the heavy-beamed lobby of the La Fonda Hotel. Sherry listened as the two dimes slithered into the box. At last the dial tone kicked in. She nodded to Hutch.

Nine-eight-nine, three-three-five-six," he read from the tattered phone book.

The steady, monotonous ringing of the phone scraped across her taut nerves. Finally someone answered.

"Santa Fe County Medical Examiner's Office," trilled a receptionist happily. "Good morning!"

"May I please speak to the chief examiner?" Her voice was husky with contained grief.

"I'm sorry, but Dr. Meadows had a late case last night. He won't be in until after lunch."

"I... I'm the mother of that late case, and I have to talk to Dr. Meadows. Could you please give me his home phone number?"

"Well," the woman said slowly, "strictly speaking, I'm not supposed to do that-"

"My daughter was eight years old," Sherry said brokenly. "I have to know what happened to her. Please."

There was a long pause from the other end of the line. "Okay, I don't think it will hurt just this one time. You can reach Dr. Meadows at nine-eight-nine, six-oh-one-three."

"Thank you," breathed Sherry as she hurriedly scribbled down the number. She hung up the receiver and Hutch silently handed her two more dimes.

The voice that answered was thick with sleep and irritation.

"Dr. Meadows?"

"Who is this?" he demanded.

"My name is Sherry Quinn. You did the autopsy on my daughter last night. I... I had to talk to you. The police told me some incredible story, and-"

"Mrs. Quinn, I'm very sorry about your little girl," Meadows said kindly, completely awake now, "but I'm afraid I can't say anything concerning the case."

"But-"

"I'm sorry, but I've been ordered to keep quiet on this, pending a complete investigation."

"What investigation? They said it was an animal attack!" Her voice was shrill with near hysteria.

"Please, Mrs. Quinn! There's nothing I can do for you." The flat buzz of a disconnected line greeted her.

"Well?" asked Hutch.

"He won't talk. The police got to him." She wrapped her arms around the cowboy's waist and clung to him as he gently stroked her golden hair. "Hutch, I've got to know."

"I understand, but what can we do now?"

"We can go to the press."

"Well, it's like this." The pretty dark-haired woman paused as she dug frantically through the welter of papers covering her battered desk. "Dammit, I lost my sandwich. Oh, here it is." She retrieved a somewhat worn-looking peanut-butter sandwich and took a big bite before continuing.

"Where was I? Oh, yeah. It's Padilla, see? He and his goon squad will probably break both your legs if you try to get in and see the autopsy report."

"But, Kathy, I have to do *something!*"

"Agreed."

"Do you think it could have been an animal attack?" Hutch asked.

"No way. We haven't had a dog, wolf, or coyote attack reported since February. I think Sherry's right. They're lying to her."

Burying her face in her hands, Sherry slumped back in the hardwood chair. Kathy Littlebird gazed with sympathy and concern at her friend. She'd met Sherry and Tom at the Santa Fe Fiesta seven years before. Soon she'd been a frequent visitor at their ranch. When cancer had claimed Tom two years ago, she'd taken vacation and spent the time seeing to it that Sherry and Pam ate, and convincing Hutch that it wouldn't be improper for him to stay on at the ranch. She had thought things were working out, and then this had hit.

She was a hardheaded Czech whose immigrant grandfather had been stuck with a literal translation of his name when he'd arrived at Ellis Island. The woman had considered changing it back, but somehow it seemed a perfect example of the bureaucratic mind. Like all of her ancestors, she was loyal and hardworking, and faced with the grief of her dear friend, there was never a question. She would get involved.

"Look, Sherry," Kathy said. "Let me do a little digging. You've given me a good description of the shape Pammy's body was in-" She bit off the words, furious with herself as Sherry flinched. "Well, anyway, I'll keep my eyes open for any other bizarre deaths in the area. Where can I reach you?"

"Back at the ranch. Life must go on, after all."

"What about the funeral?"

"The authorities refuse to release Pam's body to us." Sherry's face twisted with pain and bitterness. Hutch laid a gentle hand on her shoulder.

"Sons of bitches!" spat Kathy. "Okay, you get home and I'll let you know when I have anything."

"Thanks, Kath. You're one in a million."

"Yeah, sure." She reached for her sandwich, then drew back with disgust. A fly crawled over the brown surface of the whole-wheat bread. "Yuck! I guess I wasn't very hungry, after all."

Chapter Three

Gravel spun from beneath the wheels of the pink 1969 Mustang as it roared into the parking lot of the Big Chief Truck Stop. Debby Watkins tipped the rearview mirror and inspected her red-smeared lips. She gave her bouffant blond hair one final pat and decided that she looked like a million.

She selected a key from the mass clattering on the pink plastic key chain and unlocked the door of the diner. Her high spike heels clicked on the stained linoleum floor as she crossed to the counter. They'd come off in a couple of hours and she'd be cooking barefoot, but before that happened she wanted Ralph to see her. As she thought about the burly trucker, her hand unconsciously brushed across the red skirt where it stretched tautly across her rounded buttocks.

She slipped behind the long counter and then became aware of a low buzzing. Glancing around the rectangular white room, Debby suddenly noticed the hundreds of flies clotted in the corners of the room high up near the ceiling. Disgusted, she jerked open the closet and pulled out a broom. She propped the front door open with one of the metal and vinyl chairs, and gripping the broom like a quarter staff, she swung into battle with the insects.

They pulled sluggishly from the wall under her assault. Many dropped, smashed, to the floor under the impact of the broom, while the rest buzzed hysterically about the small restaurant. Finally the majority were dead or routed, and Debby smiled in satisfaction as she mopped the sweat from her forehead. She flipped open her large handbag and removed a bulging cosmetic case. Quickly she re-powdered her face and added another smear of blush for good measure.

Humming softly, she mixed pancake batter and took out bacon, eggs, and sausage. Ralph really liked her pancakes and always said something sweet when he came in. Not like that turd she'd married. Unloading Jesse was the best thing she'd ever done.

She set coffee on to brew and hurried to the CB radio tucked beneath the counter. Thumbing on the handset, she called breathlessly, "Breaker, breaker, are you there, Big Daddy?"

"I'm here, honey. Wheelin' right on down Eighty-five and droolin' for them 'cakes."

The gravelly voice over the speaker sent a shiver down Debby's spine, and she remembered the last evening he'd been through. It had been cramped in the bunk of the cab, but the touch of his blunt-fingered hands had made her forget the surroundings. Her mouth was suddenly dry, and she forced a giggle past the constriction in her throat.

"You real good and hungry, sugar?" she cooed. "Baby, I'm starvin', but I got this rider tucked up in the back. Besides, you don't want the bacon burnin' while we set some other things on fire."

She tittered again and rubbed her thighs together, feeling the electricity surge through her body. The heavy roar of a diesel engine in the parking lot intruded harshly into her lone fantasy.

Reluctantly she whispered back into the handset, "Ralph, sweetie, I gotta go, a customer just pulled in."

"I'll be there in fifteen. You have it hot and ready, okay?" He chuckled lewdly and cut the radio.

"Eh, *señorita*, how you doin' today?"

"Not too bad, Manuel, how about you?"

"Gas is too high, my wife is too fat, an' it's too damn hot, but other than that things are fine."

She laughed and poured coffee for the whip-lean Chicano as he slid onto a stool.

"You still seein' that big dumb Texan?"

"Yeah, what's it to you?"

"I keep tellin' you, what you need is a macho Latin lover."

"Well, if you see one, let me know, okay?" she quipped. "What will you have, Mannie? The usual?"

"*Sí.*"

She cracked three eggs over the grease-spattered grill, but her attention was centered on the parking lot. At last she heard the grinding of the gears as Ralph pulled in. Wiping her hands on the print apron, she teetered precariously to the door.

Ralph Tibbets blasted in the door, the crown of his immense cowboy hat almost brushing the frame. Whooping loudly, he tossed his hat across the room to land forgotten in one corner, and swept Debby into an embrace.

Manuel grinned appreciatively as the deep mouth-probing kiss continued. "Hey, Debby!" he yelled. "You're burnin' my eggs."

"'Hey' to you too, you stupid greaser," Tibbets shouted back. "Get your own eggs. This lady and me got business."

Debby reluctantly pulled from the circle of the big trucker's arms and returned to the grill. Tibbets sauntered to the counter, paused, then threw a mock punch at the smaller man. Manuel ducked and threw up his hands.

"Hey, man," he said, "it's like I was tellin' Debby here, I'm a lover, not a fighter."

The diner was rapidly filling with hungry men, all talking at the top of their voices. Their giant rigs stood at various angles in the dirt yard like great metal slabs of an ancient fortress. The battered metal door of the diner stood ajar, and unnoticed in the crash and rattle of dishes, the flies returned.

Ralph shoved a great forkful of pancakes into his mouth, then bellowed with laughter as Ed Morris completed his story of the truck-stop groupie he'd picked up in Vegas. He glanced down and frowned at the iridescent black-green fly busily rubbing its hairy legs on the edge of his plate.

"Son of a bitch," he muttered, taking careful aim. His massive spade-like hand swept down, flattening the insect and banging the plate into the Formica countertop. He raised his head and grinned triumphantly at the men around him, then his smile turned to an expression of fury.

A second fly, as if drawn by the destruction of its comrade, settled onto the back of Ralph's hand. It moved delicately through the hairs on the back of his hand. Irritably he shook his arm, but the insect remained firmly lodged. It swiveled its tiny, grotesque head up toward the man, and for an instant Ralph was arrested by the glittering eyes. There was an almost evil and intelligent presence embodied in the insect and, unnerved, Ralph slapped at it with his napkin.

The thin paper had little effect, and indeed, beneath the napkin's cover he felt a stabbing, burning pain. The trucker bellowed angrily and jerked away the napkin to reveal the fly's rapidly bloating body as it sucked greedily at his blood. His right hand mashed down, and with a sticky pop the insect was crushed, leaving a smear of blood on the rough skin.

Ralph was wiping vigorously at the stain when a buzzing black mass descended over his head. He screamed, his hands clawing at his eyes, as the flies thrust their sucking proboscises into the sensitive tissue of his eyes. Blood spurted from between his fingers as he staggered blindly about the diner.

Ed Morris careened into chairs and tables, seeking escape. His expensive western shirt was soaked with blood, and blood ran in rivulets from his mangled eyes. With a groan he collapsed against the white wall and slid to the floor, leaving a trail of gore in his wake.

Men ran aimlessly screaming and shouting, and over all came the hideous buzzing. Debby rushed to Ralph, desperate to help him. She flapped frantically at the attacking insects, but her fancy shoes betrayed her. Her ankle twisted and she fell to the floor, where the heavy-booted feet of her customers trampled her.

Underfoot the tile was slippery with blood. Its sticky wetness tripped the desperate victims, holding them for the flies.

Pete Balcour opened his mouth, crying for his wife. And the flies entered. They filled the warm cavity with their foul wriggling bodies and attacked the soft, pink flesh of his gums and tongue. With a moist gurgle he choked on the living mass.

When the cloud of death had begun to descend, Manuel had edged toward the door. "Holy Mary, Mother of God." He forced the words past fear-frozen lips. And for a moment it seemed she had heard him. He slithered through the deepening gore, reached the door, and leaped for the clear air beyond. But the flies had waited. They dropped from the doorjamb, clothing him in a writhing black suit of death.

She had been dreaming. It was winter, and she was with Grandpa, tramping through the deep snow. She had held his large mittened hand, and he was telling her that he loved her and that she need never go back to that house in Detroit. Suddenly great screaming black crows darted between them, beating them apart. Shivering, she awoke and wrapped skinny arms about her thin chest. Tears pricked at her eyelids and furiously she searched through the pockets of her faded Levi's for a tissue. Her search was unrewarded, and finally she gave up and wiped her nose on the hem of her dirty T-shirt.

Oh, Grandpa, she thought miserably, *why did you die? Why did you have to die?* She had been safe with the old man, but then he had gotten sick and gone to the hospital, and her mother had come and dragged her back to Detroit. She hadn't even gotten to tell him good-bye. And then had come the terrible night with her stepfather.

It had been her fifteenth birthday. As usual, there was no money for even a present, much less a party. She'd gone to bed early and lain in the sagging old bed, fighting back tears of hopelessness. Then *he* had come in. He had told her how much he loved her and how he was going to give her a present. All the time he was talking he had been dropping his pants and pulling free his engorged penis. Terrified, she'd tried to scramble from the bed, but he'd thrown himself down on her and brutally taken her. Her mother had done nothing-out of either apathy or fear. It didn't matter. That had been the end, and Charlie had ripped off her stepfather's wallet and fled. She'd been thumbing west ever since, praying that somewhere she could be happy again.

She buried her face against her knees and fought to control the ever-present tears. Suddenly she raised her head, puzzled, for the screams that had inhabited her dreams were continuing.

She wriggled down from the bunk in the cab of Ralph Tibbet's truck and peered through the open window. She gagged and recoiled as a black form careened through the open door of the diner. The man collapsed in the powdery dust of the parking lot, and from his bloody, oozing body rose a swarm of flies.

There was something almost hypnotic in the way they circled over the body of their prey. With an effort Charlie wrenched her eyes from the swirling mass. Suddenly she became aware of a tickling and then a lance of pain on her forearm. She screamed and slapped hysterically at the deeply drinking fly. Panting with terror, she flung herself across the wide seat of the truck and swiftly rolled up the windows. Outside the fragile glass barriers the flies buzzed and probed, looking for an entrance. The southwestern sun beat down on the iron coffin in which the terrified teenager waited, and within minutes the temperature began soaring.

"Oh, God, God," she muttered, "what am I gonna do?" A rivulet of sweat stung her eyes, and she realized that she had to do something. She searched frantically about the cab, each time overlooking the obvious in her terror. Only a foot away from her dangled the keys, carelessly left in the ignition by Ralph in his hurry to see Debby.

A huge knot of flies flung itself against the passenger window of the truck. With a shriek, Charlie threw herself away from the attacking black nemeses. She flung out a hand, and her fingers set the keys dancing and ringing. Sobbing with relief, she switched on the ignition, feeling the great machine leap to life beneath her.

She touched the massive gearshift, then froze. It was too big. She couldn't possibly drive it. She shook with indecision. To go or to stay. Her eyes strayed out of the broad front window and came to rest on the body already bloating in the sun-scorched lot. She gritted her teeth and, edging to the rim of the seat, stretched for the accelerator and clutch. If she almost stood, she could do it. Her thin arm shuddered with strain as she jerked the truck into gear. Hanging desperately onto the hot plastic of the wheel, she roared onto the road and away from the nightmare.

The morning sun blazed into her sweat-filmed eyes. She fought the enormous wheel, struggling to negotiate the sharp curves of the mountain road. The engine whined with the stress, for she didn't dare release even one hand from the wheel in order to shift.

The immense vehicle shuddered and rattled into yet another seemingly endless curve. The white line flashed between the eighteen wheels as Charlie strained to pull the truck into the proper lane.

She rounded the cliff face, and there directly before her chugged a tiny Volkswagen. Time slowed. Charlie stared at the white terrified face of the woman in the car and the chocolate-stained face of a young child.

The runaway swung the wheel in a desperate effort to avoid the oncoming car. The white wooden guardrail raced to meet her, and the giant rig fell slowly over the cliff into the canyon below.

For a fluttering moment she wondered about the small yellow car, then pain exploded in her hips and legs. Oh, Grandpa, she whimpered inwardly, I'm frightened. The rig settled onto its side with a groan of outraged metal. A dying behemoth with a dying human trapped inside.

Chapter Four

Kathy Littlebird stared, disgruntled, at the reproachful white sheet in the typewriter before her. She needed a story, and nothing was coming to mind. It had been a quiet night. Only two stabbings and a shooting had marred the peace of the New Mexico Sunday, and neither of those was her beat.

Snagging her battered mug, she sipped at her tea and wondered why she had brewed it. It was only eight-thirty, and already the office was sweltering. With a sigh she ambled to the chattering Teletype and skimmed the mass of paper that tumbled from the machine onto the floor. Nothing.

Another phone joined the jangling chorus that filled the office. It had a familiar sound, and Kathy ran to her desk and lifted the receiver.

"Miss Littlebird?"

"Yeah. Hi, Sammy, how are you?" She tucked the receiver beneath her chin and made herself comfortable on the corner of her desk. Sammy was one of her tipsters.

"I got a tip."

"Uh huh."

"Yeah. I think maybe it's a five-dollar tip."

A smile quirked at the corner of her generous mouth. "I'll see, Sammy, after I hear your tip. So shoot."

"There's been a big wreck up here, about twenty miles north of Española on old Eighty-five. A rig went over a cliff, and there's somebody trapped inside. I heard the cops say it was a kid."

She hated ambulance chasing and had been about to refuse to look into it, but his last sentence caught her. 'Thanks, Sammy, I'm on my way."

"Five dollars?"

"Yes, five dollars!" She dropped the receiver with a crash into its cradle and swept a notebook from her desk. Pulling open the bottom drawer, she lifted out a camera and a tape recorder. Juggling the camera, recorder, notebook, and her purse, she hurried from the building and to her small, dilapidated Datsun. She had a trip of forty or fifty miles ahead of her, and if she were going to reach the scene while there was still something to see, she'd really have to fly. She threw the car into gear and roared away from the curb. Once out of the twisting, narrow streets of Santa Fe she edged the car up to eighty and held it there. She flipped on her CB radio to monitor the state-police chatter. The last thing she needed was to get stopped for speeding.

The browns and tans of the mesas gave way to rolling hills dotted with low clumps of piñon on and juniper. Ahead the high mountains floated blue and mist-like in the clear desert air. Out of Española Littlebird turned off the interstate and onto one of the back highways of New Mexico. The engine of the Datsun began to labor as she drove higher into the mountains, and she downshifted.

She came around a curve and found the accident. Three police cars and an ambulance huddled on the lip of the canyon. A few travelers had stopped to gape stupidly over the cliffs edge at the twisted wreckage far below.

Pulling onto the shoulder, Kathy switched off the engine. She stepped from the car and hurried to the trunk. She always carried a pair of rugged shoes for an emergency such as this one. As she tightened the knot on the ankle-high boots, she reflected that she must look like

Mammy Yokum in her Anne Klein skirt and hiking boots. Gathering up her equipment, she pushed through the crowd and began the treacherous climb into the canyon below.

The mammoth eighteen-wheeler was lying on its side, the driver's door down. Two patrolmen attacked the passenger door of the cab with crowbars. Sweat formed dark halos beneath their armpits, and one maintained a steady mumble of invective as he worked. Captain Padilla stood behind the laboring men, shouting inane instructions that were for the most part ignored.

Keeping a wary eye on the Spanish policeman, Kathy slipped to the other side of the truck where a young ambulance driver lay full length on the ground, and murmured encouragement to the person inside.

"How is he?" Kathy whispered.

"He? It's a girl in there," responded the driver. His brown eyes were dark with worry.

Kathy flopped down on the dusty clay, heedless of her new skirt. From inside the cab there came a series of tiny whimpers like a small animal, hurt, trapped, and dying. Kathy peered through the cracked windshield and could just make out the tear and blood-streaked face of a teenage girl.

"Sweetie, can you hear me?" she called gently.

There was an almost imperceptible nod of the brown head. "They're going to get you out. You just hang on, okay?" Kathy paused, feeling callous for what she was about to do. She shook off the emotion and set her tape recorder near the window.

"Honey, what happened? Why were you trying to drive this truck?"

The ambulance driver gripped her shoulder, pulling her harshly to a sitting position. "What the hell are you doing? That kid is dying in there," he whispered tensely.

"And that's why I've got to talk to her now." She

knocked the man's hand aside and dropped once more to the hard ground.

"I'm back," she called to the girl. "My name is Kathy, and I'm a journalist. Do you think you can talk to me?"

"Y-yes. Have to..." The teenager gasped out the words. A transparent red bubble oozed from the girl's lips and burst with a moist popping sound. The blood trickled slowly down her chin. Kathy squeezed her eyes shut for an instant, then returned her attention to the girl.

"They... they're all... dead. They killed them... all." The dark little head began to whip from side to side in terror and anguish as the girl forced out the words.

"Who?" Kathy cried. "Who's dead?"

"Ralph." She gulped in air. "He... he was nice to me." Tears were flowing down the girl's face once more, but her arms were trapped and she couldn't wipe them away. "The flies," she suddenly moaned. "Flies... flies ate them all!"

Kathy and the driver exchanged puzzled looks. "Flies?" Littlebird repeated.

"Awful! Buzzing blackness. Ate them! Ate them all." The child's voice rose to a hysterical shriek. The girl choked on a great gout of thick red blood that pumped from her mouth.

Suddenly Kathy was seized by the collar and pulled to her feet. Padilla stood over her, his face engorged with rage. "What in the hell are you doin' here?"

"I'm a journalist. Where else should I be?" Kathy muttered resentfully. She massaged her throat where the collar of her blouse had cut into the tender skin.

Padilla glanced down at the softly humming recorder. He smiled grimly, his eyes narrowing to slits in his fleshy face, and he lifted one cowboy-booted foot.

"Hey!" Littlebird protested, but he brought his heel down onto the fragile device. Plastic splintered and tape spun crazily from the cassette.

"You're going to pay for that one, Padilla," Kathy raged as she knelt in the dirt and plucked ineffectually at the tangled tape.

"Gosh, Kathy. I'm sorry about that, but if you leave things lying around on the ground, accidents are bound to happen. Isn't that so?" he asked the ambulance driver with an innocent grin, but his eyes were like flint.

"Uh... uh, yeah," stuttered the driver, his eyes flicking from Kathy to the state-police captain.

The pretty journalist ground her teeth with frustration. There was nothing she could do as long as Padilla claimed it was an accident and had a witness to back him up. It didn't matter that he'd intimidated the driver into it.

Padilla's contrite expression faded into a snarl of anger. His beefy forefinger hammered at her shoulder, driving her back from the truck.

"'You're interfering with police officers at their job, got it? Now clear out of here, and I better not see anything in that sewer you call a paper about this accident, got it?"

"You ever hear of the Constitution, Padilla? Or hasn't it made it into Marvel Comics yet? You can't get away with this. You and your bully boys can't silence the press. There's something funny going on and I'm going to get to the bottom of it!" She glared up into his brown moon face. The captain sucked in air through his nose, and the tendons in his neck swelled with fury. His spade-like hand settled onto the butt of his service pistol, and Kathy took a hasty step back.

"You keep pushin'," he growled, "and you may be looking for another job in another state. Things happen to people who get too nosy," he concluded softly. His small black eyes, almost hidden in rolls of fat, stared at the expensive German camera that hung from her shoulder. Reaching out, he jerked the camera from her arm and, spinning it over his head by the strap, flung it into the trunk of a nearby pine tree. Littlebird's protest died in her throat at the expression on the burly captain's face.

"Did she tell you anything?" he asked, jerking his thumb at the cab of the truck.

"N-no," replied Kathy, backing carefully away. "No, nothing."

"Good. Just see to it that you don't remember anything. Now clear out." He stomped away, and Kathy stared bleakly at the ruins of her camera and recorder. With a sigh she turned back to the driver, who was looking at her with sympathy and embarrassment.

"Hey, it's okay. It's not in your job description to handle gorillas."

"I'm sorry I can't help you, but I'd lose my job."

Her mouth twisted as if at a bad taste. "The crony system in this part of the state is unbelievable, so I understand." She started to walk away, then turned back. "Say, what's your name?"

"Devon McNee."

"If I call, will you tell me what happens to the little girl?"

"Sure."

"Okay, I'll be in touch."

"You still here?" She turned to face Padilla. "Well, maybe a lady like you just needs to be escorted back to her car." His voice was thick with sarcasm. "Eh, Montoya?"

"*Sí*, Captain." One of the crowbar wielders hurried around the truck.

"See to it that this *lady* gets to her car. And make sure that she drives away in it, *comprendes?*"

"*Sí*, Captain."

Sourly Kathy wondered if Padilla had all of his patrolmen trained to use only two words. Montoya took her firmly by the arm and propelled her back up the cliff face. Reaching the top, she looked back as the door of the cab fell away and McNee tenderly lifted a broken form from the wreckage. Then the patrolman roughly pulled her to her car and thrust her in.

"Now beat it!" he said in a credible imitation of his boss.

"Oh, Officer," she said sweetly. "Tell Padilla that he better pray to God for his soul, 'cause his ass belongs to me. I'm going to get the answers, and a nice little cover-up like this ought to be just the thing we need to get him out of office."

The state trooper pushed his hat back on his head and stared at her, a puzzled expression on his plump face.

"Never mind, dear," Kathy said, patting him gently on the cheek. Waste of a good speech, she thought regretfully as she pulled away.

Kathy returned the phone to its cradle and stared thoughtfully and sadly into space. The girl had died during the long ambulance ride back to Española. Devon had said that she continued to babble about flies before she slipped into a coma. Kathy remembered the pain-dazed eyes that had gazed beseechingly out at her, and she shivered.

She pressed the tips of her fingers against her eyes and reviewed yet again the strange words the girl had spoken. It was clear the girl had seen something... but what? Somewhere there were people lying dead, killed by something so hideous that the teenager's conscious mind could not deal with it. But why come up with flies as personae for the mysterious killer? The journalist shook her head. It just didn't make any sense.

Suddenly Sherry's description of Pammy's body came back to her. Her friend had told her that Pammy looked as if she'd been chewed on, but not by an animal with teeth. Kathy wondered if there could be a connection between Pamela's death and whatever the girl in the truck had seen. It didn't seem likely, but she had promised she'd call Sherry if she discovered anything, no matter how unlikely. With a sigh she lifted the receiver once more.

The phone began to ring with that distant hollow sound that rural calls often have. Kathy hung on grimly ring after ring and hoped that Sherry wasn't up on one of the high ranges. At last she heard Sherry's voice at the other end of the line.

"Hello?"

"Hi, it's me." Kathy heard the neighing of a horse in the background and realized that Sherry was using the phone in the barn. "Where have you been?"

"Giving one of our young bulls an injection. It wasn't something I could leave in the middle."

"I can appreciate that." Littlebird laughed. "How are you doing?" she asked, her laughter fading.

"Holding up," Sherry replied shortly. "Do you have anything for me?"

"I'm not certain, but I did run across something a little strange today."

"Oh?"

"Yeah. An eighteen-wheeler went off a cliff north of Española this morning. When I got up there, instead of finding the usual brawny trucker inside, there was this tiny girl. Fourteen or fifteen at the most. Anyway she told me this incredible story. Apparently wherever she'd come from she saw some people killed in a rather hideous fashion. She claimed that they were attacked and 'eaten' by flies. Now, remember she was badly hurt and it could all have been hallucination. I feel sort of silly calling you, but you said to tell you if I heard anything out of the ordinary, and believe me, this was certainly out of the ordinary."

There was a long pause while Sherry digested Kathy's information. "That does sound sort of crazy and wild. I know dogs didn't kill Pammy, but flies..."

"Yeah, I know. It seemed a little off the wall to me too. Well, listen, I'd better run. I've still got to get something into tomorrow's edition, and that gorilla Padilla warned me not to write anything about the accident. I think I'll go talk to Al and see if he's up to bearding the state police."

"That seems rather odd," Sherry said thoughtfully. "Why should Padilla care if you write a story?"

Kathy paused, considering. "Yeah, you're right, it does seem odd."

"Also a little familiar," added Sherry. "Remember how they put a lid on Pammy's death. They wouldn't even let us handle the burial arrangements." Her voice was suddenly thick with tears.

Kathy was torn by the quaver in her friend's voice, and she damned the cosmos because it was only Tuesday. "Look, I'll try to get up and see you one of these weekends, okay?"

"I hope you can. I... I'd like to have somebody to talk to. Hutch is a dear, but another woman would be nice."

"I'll be there," Kathy promised her friend, and hung up.

Sherry replaced the receiver and stared bleakly at the scrawled messages on the weathered gray wood of the barn next to the phone. "Four tons of grain, due Tuesday." Her husband's bold script leaped off the wall to taunt her. She felt tears prick at her eyelids and she furiously blinked them away.

Her family was gone, torn from her with almost diabolical cruelty. Tom wasting away in the V.A. Hospital in Albuquerque, and Pammy, bloody and disfigured, lying in the dust of the corral. Sherry felt like a figure from Greek tragedy, a Fury perhaps who had been loosed upon the world to seek vengeance. But unfortunately she had nothing to strike out against.

Thrusting her hands into the pockets of her Levi's, she scuffed down the wide center aisle of the barn watching the sawdust fly up before the toes of her boots. Heads were thrust over stall doors, and she absently patted each horse as she made her way into the sunlight.

Hutch, stripped to the waist, climbed over the old field tractor, tinkering and tuning, getting it ready for another hay-mowing. Sherry watched the play of muscles in his bronzed back as he threw open the hood of the machine and reached with one grease-stained hand deep into the engine. The sight of him alive and strong helped to drive away the ghosts who had come whispering to join her in the darkness of the barn.

Straightening, he wiped his hands on a dirty rag and noticed Sherry standing silently in the door of the barn. His slow crooked grin lit his features, and he walked to her with the rolling gait of the born horseman.

"You look like you need to talk."

"Kathy just called."

"Did she have anything interestin' for us?"

Sherry started to shake her head, then stopped. Maybe it was crazy, but she wanted Hutch's opinion on the story she'd just heard. "I'm not sure."

"Let's take a break and go up to the house. You can tell me about it over a lemonade."

"That's the best offer I've had all day." She smiled warmly up at him.

Arm in arm, they walked up the hill to the old adobe. The corral, scene of Pammy's hideous death, had been torn down, but Sherry still averted her eyes from the spot. Hutch pressed her closer to his side, feeling her wordless pain.

He scrubbed his hands in the kitchen sink while Sherry poured two tall glasses of lemonade. With a sigh they both sank down at the table. He drained the glass in one long draft, then, drawing the back of his hand across his mouth, leaned back in his chair. "Okay, shoot."

"Kathy was checking out an accident earlier in the day. The victim was a young girl who'd wrecked a big rig."

"You mean as in truck?"

"Yeah, apparently one of those eighteen-wheelers."

"What the hell was a kid doin' drivin' a truck?"

"I don't know, I guess Kathy never found out. The strange thing, though, was the story the girl told. Kathy said she wasn't making a lot of sense, but the girl seemed to be saying that some people somewhere had been killed by a bunch of flies."

Hutch stared at her incredulously for several seconds. "Well, I know they're pretty bad this time of year, but, honey, that's just plain ridiculous."

"That's what I thought." She sighed and stared down at her brown hands where they cupped the icy glass. "I just wish we could find *something*. I'd even settle for killer flies if I could only know what killed her. I can accept anything if I can understand it." Her voice had dropped so low Hutch strained to hear her final words.

He gazed lovingly at her bent head. Her honey-gold hair had fallen forward like a shining veil to hide her delicate oval face. As he watched, a tear fell onto the polished wood of the table and lay glistening on the grainy surface. That single tear broke his control. For days—no, for years, he'd been trying to keep to his place, to be a gentleman, but now Sherry was hurting and he had to help her. He rose and crossed quietly to her. His big, rough hand awkwardly began to stroke her hair.

He rested his hand on her slender shoulder and felt it trembling with grief. Suddenly she wrenched about in the chair and buried her face against his chest. Her arms snaked around his waist, clinging desperately to him.

His shirt was becoming damp from her tears, but

it didn't matter. She was in his arms, and her sweet scent filled his nostrils. He caught her chin in one hand and forced her head up. For a long moment they remained frozen; then slowly, lovingly, he bent his head and captured her lips with his.

At first she was passive beneath the gentle probings of his lips and tongue, but then she awakened. Her small tongue darted in and out of his mouth, fencing and teasing with his.

He pulled her to her feet and pressed her against his hard body. She gave a gasp and arched closer. The taste of her was like fine whiskey, and had the same effect. His head felt light and he could feel the blood pounding in his temples. When Tom was alive, she'd been his woman, and Hutch had never raised his eyes to her, but in her widowhood she had come to fill his dreams, and he longed for her. Now she was in his arms, and his body responded with a violence that amazed even him.

Her hands clutched frantically at his hair, holding his mouth in place so she could drink ever deeper.

With a groan he lifted her into his arms and walked down the hall to her room.

The shutters had been closed against the afternoon sun, and the darkness of the heavy carved beams and the whitewashed adobe walls lent the room a welcome coolness. Her wide Spanish-style bed beckoned, and he laid her gently on top of the Navajo blanket that served as a bedspread.

He stretched out beside her and continued his exploration of her body. Slowly he opened her blouse to reveal her taut breasts, unencumbered by a brassiere. He dropped his head and teased each pink-brown nipple into life with his lips and tongue.

Suddenly he froze and raised his head. He looked into her deep blue eyes and felt guilt. This had been her and Tom's bed.

"Sherry, honey. I'm sorry... I can... I mean-"

Her hand traced a languid line from his temple to his jaw. "Hutch, shut up," she whispered with a smile as she unbuttoned his shirt. "Don't talk. Love me."

He stood and quickly pulled off his faded and dusty Levi's. The woman executed a sensual dance on the bed as she wriggled from her tight jeans. He rejoined her on the bed and began an intimate tour of her body with mouth and hands. Her nails raked his back and she moaned, whipping her head from side to side on the pillow. She caressed his thighs and cupped his erect penis in both hands.

He was shaking with his need for her, yet he held back, determined to give her the maximum pleasure before he sought his own release.

"Hutch," she cried, arching passionately against him. "I need you! I want you!".

He entered her. Slowly at first, then faster as a rhythm as old as time took control of both of them, they moved together. He exploded within her, and with a cry they fell back, to lie exhausted on the bed.

Sherry murmured drowsily and nuzzled closer to his broad chest. He watched as her lids fell over her blue eyes and she slept. He brushed a tendril of hair from her forehead and watched the steady rise and fall of her bosom.

Well, if nothing else, he'd made it possible for her to sleep, he thought. And he slept too, happy and peaceful in the knowledge that she needed him. Perhaps even as much as he needed her.

Chapter Five

The sunlight played across the tumbled bed, highlighting the sweat-slick bodies of the two people on the bed. The boy, his bold black eyes glittering with anticipation, fell onto the girl where she reclined against the pillows.

"Ah, Quintana, no," she protested, giggling. "We've done it once already, and it is Sunday."

"So?" muttered the young man, biting even harder at her neck and bosom.

She caught his head in her hands, forcing him to look at her. "But we should be at Mass." Her full red lips pouted provocatively at him.

"I worship at another altar today, María."

Her brown eyes filled with apprehension at his words. "No, Quintana, you must not say such a thing. It is blasphemous. Something might happen to us." Her voice fell to a superstitious whisper. Unsteadily she lifted her waist-length black hair and flung it over her bare shoulders. For an instant the boy seemed affected by his lover's words, but he squared his shoulders and his eyes raked the small room as if daring some otherworldly power to appear.

"There, you see, María. There is nothing to fear. The priests are old men who try to keep the young from their joys with words of fear and death. Now come."

Meekly she obeyed, sliding back down into the bed and opening her arms to his caresses. His rough, work-hardened hands swept over her body, probing, parting her warm thighs, exploring the very heart of her. She moaned with pleasure and the tendons in her neck stood etched and taut as she arched to meet him.

Suddenly she felt the touch of insects crawling over her legs. With a shriek of disgust she wrenched from the boy's arms and flapped with both hands at the flies that had settled on her. The insects rose briefly from her damp flesh, only to settle quickly back. Her fresh blood beckoned them, and they drove their sucking proboscises deep into her skin. The boy beat at the insects, but soon he too fell victim to the sucking, stinging nightmare. Abandoned to the flies, María cried in agony as the flies ate her alive.

Through blood-smeared eyes María stared in horror as the flies stabbed and sucked at her lover's groin. He beat frantically at them as his screams faded to harsh groans. The flies continued to feed on the soft tissue of his manhood.

It was her last sight before her world narrowed to one of blood and pain. And at last she saw nothing at all.

Johnny Santiago ran a soft cloth once more over the tiny chain-link steering wheel in his shiny red Chevrolet. Two weeks' pay it had cost him, but it was worth it, for now the car was almost perfect. He had the special hydraulics system that enabled him to make the car dance, and a horn that played "La Cucaracha." The dashboard and the seats were covered with thick black fur and a large rosary swung from the rearview mirror.

He checked his watch. Christ, it was ten-thirty. If Nina didn't hurry, they wouldn't get a good place for the drive through town. He glanced across the heat-baked plaza to the church. A few people were emerging from the great carved wood doors. Mass was over.

The worshipers were almost entirely women and children, and a few old men. The young men had their cars, and their work. They had no time for the priests and the church.

A slim girl skipped happily through the doors. She paused to remove her mantilla while her eyes searched the plaza. He felt his heart constrict at the sight of her, so beautiful in her pink dress.

She spotted the car and waved vigorously. She slipped out of her high-heeled sandals and ran across the plaza. Johnny leaned across the car to open the passenger door. She slid in and pressed a kiss on his lips.

"Johnny, you should have come. Father Austin had many fine words to say."

"According to you, Father Austin *always* has many fine words to say," he teased, watching the way her unusual blue eyes sparkled with excitement. "Besides," he added. "Why do you want me to go to church so badly?"

She tossed her head and the short black curls danced about her heart-shaped face. "Because I want you to be a good man. A man worthy to be the father of my children."

"I am that man," he cried, outraged.

"No," she said seriously, shaking her head. "You still love this car and your buddies more than you love me and the home we would make."

"But, Nina, I want to marry you!"

"When you have become a man," she said firmly.

He glowered over the chain-link wheel that only minutes before had given him such pleasure. There was a lot of truth in what she said, and it hurt.

"Come on, let's not fight. Let's go and parade so everyone can see that beautiful new steering wheel." His face brightened. "Oh, *si"*

They drove to the bottom of the hill below the plaza and joined the thirty other cars already there. Young men compared their machines while their women reapplied lipstick, combed and teased their hair, and gossiped.

Fifteen minutes later they had formed their line. The weekly low-rider parade in Moscón, New Mexico, was about to begin.

* * * * *

"Pattie, will you shut up!" The three-year-old's wails became even louder in the confines of the station wagon.

"Mildred, for God's sake, I can't think, much less drive with that howling." The plump face of the man was shiny with sweat, and his hands clenched and unclenched on the slippery wheel as they raced down the highway.

"I'm doing the best I can." The querulous voice grated on him, rasping down his already taut nerves.

"You're the one who wanted to bring the baby," he reminded her tightly.

"Well, I didn't know you were bringing us to the end of the world. Why couldn't we have gone to Mother's in Florida?" the woman whined.

"Because I'm *sick* of Florida, and I've never been West and I wanted to see it."

"You're always thinking just of yourself, I don't know why I married you," she sobbed over the sobs of her child.

It was an old argument, circular and impossible to settle. The man ignored her. Instead, he pulled out a handkerchief and mopped sweat from his face and neck. He thought savagely of what he would say to the car-rental dealer when they got back to Albuquerque. To have the air-conditioning go out in the middle of a desert in July!

He gunned the car up a long grade, ignoring the speed-limit signs and the sign that proclaimed "MOSCÓN, New Mexico. Population 2023." He roared into the plaza and slammed on his brakes to avoid rear-ending the slow-moving car in front of him. Sticking his head out of the window, he stared at a seemingly endless line of cars all creeping and bouncing down the streets surrounding the plaza.

"Wanna drink," whimpered his child.

"Joe, would you hurry up!"

"I can't. These goddamn Mexicans have me blocked," he answered, pulling his head back in the window.

"I thought you just *loved* the Spanish culture," his wife said sarcastically.

"Mildred, I'm warning you," he gritted.

"Wanna drink!" screamed Pattie from the backseat. He flinched from the noise.

"Dammit, Joe. Stop this car. I'm getting out and Pattie and I are going to get something to eat!"

"I can't! I'm hemmed in by these cars." The three-year-old's screams lanced through his head, settling into a stabbing pain behind his eyes. He pounded furiously on the steering wheel, then began to blare the horn.

Over the blare of his and other horns Joe Weinstein became aware of a piercing buzz. Puzzled, he glanced down at the dashboard, wondering if it were the car signaling some new failure. Everything appeared normal.

He lifted his eyes to the road, to discover that the windshield was covered by a mass of crawling black bodies. He was repulsed by the sight of millions of hairy legs rubbing incessantly together. Wildly he turned on the windshield wipers. The twin blades battered at the bloated bodies, sweeping them from the glass.

The flies gathered and shot through the open windows of the station wagon. They settled onto his face, a seething foul mass of decay and sucking proboscises. Agony ran through his body as the sharp proboscises drove deep into the delicate tissue of his mouth and lips.

A sound, no longer human, was torn from his throat as the flies blinded him, drinking deeply of the precious eye fluids. In his last agony, Joe threw his arms over his head, his foot driving hard onto the accelerator. The car careened across the tree-dotted plaza with its bandstand and cannon, crashing at last into the thick trunk of a cottonwood.

Mildred beat frantically at the insects that covered her child, devouring her alive, but it was no use. Within moments she had joined the child as an unrecognizable black and red mass on the seat of the wrecked car.

Johnny flipped the toggle switch that controlled the car's hydraulic system. The back of the car rose high into the air; then with another flick of the switch, it fell, bouncing to within inches of the pavement. He grinned at Nina, who smiled back indulgently.

Suddenly he frowned, for the cars ahead of him had begun to weave erratically onto the sidewalks. He swerved hard to the right to avoid his friend Pepito, whose blue-and-silver Ford had almost sideswiped him.

"Hey," he yelled, but the rest of his words died in his throat, for Pepito's face was a writhing black horror. He gaped stupidly at the bizarre, nightmarish sight as the flies gathered for the assault. Nina saw the buzzing cloud approaching, and breaking the grip of terror that held her frozen, she hit the electric-window button.

They would not close in time, she screamed inwardly-as she watched in fascination as the flies drew near. With a sigh the windows slid into place, and the attacking insects smashed into the unyielding glass. A few had managed to enter the car, but she ignored their bites and beat them to death with her missal.

"Johnny!" She gripped his shoulder and shook him hard. "Johnny, you must get us out of here!"

"I can't," he muttered hoarsely. "I'm trapped."

"Then go across the plaza."

He stared at her in horror. "But... but I would tear up my car. Hey, man, no way could I do that."

She had to shout to be heard over the whine of the flies. "Which is more important, your car or our lives? Johnny, we are going to die. Only you can save us." He gazed down into her beautiful pleading face and suddenly pictured it crawling with bugs. He wrenched the wheel over and plowed over the curb and across the plaza. There was a horrible ripping, grinding sound as the shockless car tore out its underside.

As they sped through the tiny village, they saw people-neighbors, family-staggering from their homes, gore running from their faces. They wanted to stop, to help, but they could do nothing, and they knew it. Still their cowardice ate at them, and their guilt. At last the highway stretched before them. Johnny pressed the accelerator to the floor and they raced for Santa Fe.

Marcelino Sánchez snored loudly in the mud of the alley behind Tito's Bar. The flies dropped quietly onto his outflung arm. From his wrist to his elbow there ran an oozing sore, and the female flies dug deep into the warm, welcoming environment, depositing their load of eggs. But Marcelino Sánchez slept on.

He awakened suddenly, his mouth dry, almost cracking from his thirst. He pushed to a sitting position, resting his back against the mud wall of the bar, and tried to think. Jesús, María, he felt so sick. He held his head in his filthy hands and tried to remember where he was.

He had left Tito's last night to relieve himself. Lifting red-rimmed eyes, he looked blankly about the alley. He tried to concentrate, but the throbbing pain in his arm made it difficult. He probed at the angry burn with muddy fingers. He had gotten it when a pan of chili had been knocked from the stove.

He frowned and rubbed at his face. The stubble rasped across his hand. Funny, the burn had been feeling better, but now it hurt as if a fire had been lit inside of it.

A chill shook him and he rolled over onto his side. Cramps seized him and he vomited into the mud. Gripping the wall with his good hand, he pulled himself to his feet. The effort left him gasping, and nausea rose once more. He inched along the wall to the back door of the bar and hammered desperately on the peeling surface. No answer.

The pain was increasing. Soon Marcelino knew he would not be able to walk.

"Madre de Dios," he prayed through lips that were cracked and bleeding from the fever that raged through his body.

Help. He had to have help. He pushed away from the support of the wall and staggered drunkenly toward the street.

The village was silent. Marcelino saw cars lying like dead animals. His foot struck something soft and yielding, and he fell facedown onto the hard cement of the sidewalk. Moaning with pain, he pushed back onto one knee and stared in disbelief at the body that had tripped him.

He blinked at the corpse and tried to fathom why a body would be lying on the street. He poked at the body, which lay on its side, and succeeded in rolling it onto its back.

Bloody eye sockets stared grotesquely at the serene blue sky. The old man vomited again. Bile dripped from his chin and onto his ragged flannel shirt. He peered about the plaza, and everywhere he looked were the dead.

Terrified, he lurched to his feet and tried to run from the nightmare. His pain was so great that he moaned with every breath. The inflamed skin of his burned arm began to undulate as if it possessed a life of its own. He stared in horror as the soft red skin peeled back, bursting open with the pressure from the creatures emerging from their foul womb.

White and wriggling, the larvae erupted from his arm. A scream was torn from his throat. It echoed through the silent streets. The dying cry of a dying village.

Chapter Six

"Oh, Charles," Kathy Littlebird said, sighing, as she sank gratefully into the chair at the Bull Ring, one of Santa Fe's most elegant restaurants.

"What, dear?" asked Dr. Charles Edwards, a faint smile crossing his normally dour face.

"What a day I've had!"

"Ummm?" he murmured, handing her a menu and a drink.

She ignored the menu, but quickly grabbed the glass of sherry.

"Typical journalist," he teased.

Kathy glared at him over the rim of the glass, then softened and brushed his cheek with the back of her hand. "Actually, I've never needed a drink more in my life."

"How so?"

"I've spent the entire day fighting with the state police. I know they're hiding something, but I can't get a lead on what."

"Do I know the reason for this crusade, or is this a new one?" Edwards asked, offering the menu once more. It was again ignored.

"I think this is a new one," Kathy admitted.

She was very close to the slight, middle-aged doctor, and they had enjoyed a very rewarding affair for some two years now. Unfortunately their busy careers did tend to keep them apart more than they liked, especially since he lived in Los Alamos and she in Santa Fe.

"Do you remember my friend Sherry?" she asked, picking up the thread of the conversation.

"Yes, a pretty blond who runs a ranch up north, right?"

"Uh huh, that's the one. Well, last week her little girl was killed."

"That's very tragic."

"It's not only tragic, it's weird. The official autopsy gave the cause of death as 'animal attack,' but Sherry and Hutch... her ranch-hand," she explained, seeing Charles' lost expression. "Anyway, when she and Hutch came to see me, they said there were no signs of bites on her body. She was apparently a bloody mess, but there were *no* teeth marks."

Edwards paused, his water glass halfway to his mouth. "How very odd," he murmured. "Did they give you any more information?"

"Uh huh, they said that Pammy looked as if the skin had been punctured in thousands of places so that there was almost no whole skin left."

Pulling thoughtfully at his lower lip, Edwards considered Kathy's vivacious face for several moments before speaking. "Funny, I had a case with precisely those sort of symptoms about twelve days ago."

"What?" Littlebird shouted.

"Kathy, please," admonished the doctor with a pained expression, as curious and outraged diners stared at them.

"Sorry," she muttered contritely, "but this is the first lead I've had. The only other thing that looked promising turned out to be science fiction." There was a discreet cough to her right. Their waiter had returned.

"I'll have the trout amandine, and the lady will have the veal," Edwards said smoothly.

"I will?" asked Kathy with a bewildered glance at

her untouched menu.

"You will," repeated the doctor firmly.

"Okay, what case?" she demanded after the waiter had left.

"One of the truck drivers for the labs, a young fellow named Josh Gatlin, was brought into Emergency a week ago Tuesday. He was dead on arrival, but it wasn't the accident that killed him."

"Accident?"

"Sorry, I'm getting ahead of myself. He was making a run down to Albuquerque when his truck hit a cow. The only injury he sustained from the wreck was a broken leg, but he died from massive blood loss and terrible wounds over his entire body, exactly as you described your friend's child."

Kathy meditatively spun her sherry glass, watching the small circular, depression it formed in the white tablecloth. It was pure journalistic hunch, but she decided to play it.

"What was he carrying in that truck?"

"Be glad it wasn't classified, or we'd both be in trouble for that question," remarked Edwards. "Fortunately I can answer, for all the good it will do you. He was transporting a load of flies."

"Flies!"

"Yes, they were on their way to California."

"Do you know who was in charge of this project?"

"No, but if it's important I can find out."

"It is, Charles, believe me, it is." She closed her eyes, hearing again the words of a dying child. "Buzzing blackness. Flies! The flies ate them all!"

"Charles," she said softly as she opened her eyes. "I don't want to sound like an alarmist or anything, but I think our lives may depend upon it."

"Hutch," called Sherry. "It's Kathy, and she's got something for us." He hurried into the kitchen and placed his head next to hers so they could both listen.

"Sherry, I've got a lead on another death that *strongly* resembles Pammy's. The guy was a truck driver for the Los Alamos labs, and get this-he was carrying a load of *flies*"

Sherry and Hutch exchanged incredulous looks, remembering the call Kathy had made to them only two days before concerning the dying teenager.

"Say again?" asked Hutch, taking the phone from Sherry.

"Yes, you really heard right," Kathy said, her voice tinged with impatience. "Flies."

"We've got to get up to the lab," Sherry yelled into the mouthpiece.

"Before you rush off half-cocked, let me finish. The guy in charge of the fly project is named Fonseca."

"Kathy, you're a wonder! How did you ever find out?" Sherry asked.

"Sources, dearie, sources."

Hutch laughed at the smug self-satisfied tone. "We're goin' now, Kathy. If you need us you can find Sherry and me at the labs."

"Good luck, and keep me posted. I expect a scoop out of this."

"You've got it." Sherry laughed.

"Is she crazy or are we, for listening to her?" asked Hutch as he hung up the phone.

"I don't think so, Hutch. I mean, think about it for a minute. You know all the projects they work on up on that mountain. That's where they developed the atom bomb. Isn't it possible that they came up with a strain of..."

"Killer flies?" finished Hutch.

"Sounds pretty silly when you say it out loud like that." She leaned against a flour-strewn worktable. "Oh, Hutch, I just did so want it to be a real lead."

The quaver in her voice lanced through him like a

physical pain. Even though it was a wild-goose chase, he decided they'd make the trip to Los Alamos. Even if they found no answers, at least Sherry would be doing something.

"I'll call Bill and have him watch the stock while we're gone."

"Thank you," she said simply, taking his hands in hers. "I know it may be useless, but it's the only chance we've got. If this doesn't work out, we may as well give up."

"No, we're not givin' up. We're gonna find out what killed Pammy and lay that ghost to rest." Quietly she rested her head against his chest.

They set out in the predawn, trying to beat the heat of the day, and by eight o'clock they were winding up the narrow road leading to the high plateau upon which rested Los Alamos. They met almost no traffic on the climb up the mountain, for Los Alamos was a basically closed city. The people who lived there also worked there, and only on the weekends would they venture down to Santa Fe or Albuquerque seeking entertainment. The work of the lab was varied, ranging from weapons development to the medical use of mesons, or the invention of a working ion drive for spaceships.

The couple rounded a final curve and before them loomed the massive concrete guard tower. No guards stepped out to block their entrance, but Sherry couldn't prevent a shiver from running down her spine.

Hutch slowed the pickup to a discreet twenty-five miles an hour. He had a feeling that a speeding ticket in Los Alamos would be handled by the FBI, and he didn't want a chance to find out. They stopped to ask directions at a filling station, and soon they had pulled up in front of the administration building for the Los Alamos Scientific Laboratories.

They entered the bunkerlike building, their boot

heels loud on the tile floor. Sherry halted before a bored receptionist.

"Yes?" the tone was cold, and the pinched-faced woman scarcely lifted her eyes from the telephone message pad before her.

"My name is Sherry Quinn, and I'd like to see Dr. Fonseca."

"Is he expecting you?"

"No, but this is very important."

"We do not like to have our scientists disturbed by casual visitors. I would suggest that you call and arrange for an appointment."

Hutch started forward, but Sherry's slim hand caught him in the chest, holding him in place. Her eyes were blue fire and her face was white with anger.

"I've driven over eighty miles this morning, and I'm quite desperate. That means that I'm perfectly capable of making a scene that really will disturb your scientists. Now, either you get Dr. Fonseca on the phone, or I'm going to your superior even if that means that I walk over your face to do it."

Hutch folded his arms across his chest and watched with amusement while the slender ranchwoman laid out the tight-ass bitch. For Hutch's money Sherry in her faded Levi's, her hair hanging straight and free to her shoulders, was far lovelier than the polished creature with her perfectly manicured nails and sculptured hair. And obviously much tougher, he added to himself, for the receptionist hurriedly grabbed the phone and put through a call to Fonseca's office.

In a few minutes a young man in a white lab coat hurried into the reception area. "'Mrs. Quinn?"

"Yes."

"If you'll follow me, please. I'm Dr. Berkeley, Dr. Fonseca's assistant," he said as they fell into step with him. The young man held open a heavy metal door and they stepped through into a wide hall punctuated with gray windowless doors.

"Is it okay for us to be back here?" asked Hutch nervously.

"Oh, yes, this isn't a restricted area. The work done here is non-classified, so you can come in. You will have to wear visitors' badges, though. I obtained a couple from Security on my way down here." He handed the couple two large red plastic badges with VISITOR printed in bold black letters in the center.

Berkeley then led them up a flight of stairs and down another long hall. He stopped before one of the featureless doors and pushed it open. The white walls and floor of the inner room seemed blinding after the dull gray of the outer hall. Cages of mice, aquariums of frogs, and cages of birds filled the room. Perched on a high stool before a worktable was a heavyset man with graying hair. He lifted his head at their entrance and skewered Sherry with the most piercing gaze she'd ever seen. His eyes were a strange topaz color and complemented his swarthy skin.

"Dr. Fonseca, these are the people who were asking for you."

Sherry hung back, intimidated by the mysteriously technical setting. Fonseca seemed to sense her unease, for he rose with a warm smile and, crossing to her, extended his hand.

"I'm Robert Fonseca. I'm very pleased to meet you, Mrs. Quinn, although I admit I'm at a loss as to why you'd seek me out."

"I appreciate your time, Doctor. What I wanted was some information about the fly experiments you were doing."

He gave her a sharp look. "It's funny you should mention that project because in a sense it was a dismal failure, and I'm back to square one with it."

"How so?"

"Well, when the truck crashed, tragically killing

that young man, all of my flies escaped, so I don't know if they can do what I bred them to do."

"And what was that, Doctor?"

"My field is recombinant DNA-"

"Pardon?" said Hutch, turning from his scrutiny of a cage of small white mice.

"Genetic engineering," Fonseca explained. "I had developed what I hoped were a strain of superflies."

"Why?" interrupted Hutch again, his rancher's sense outraged by the concept.

"No, no, not for the reasons you think. These flies were designed to kill fruit flies, and they were on their way to California. Since we don't have fruit flies in New Mexico, you can see why my experiment was a failure. I don't know if my creations are killers or not."

"I think you can assume they are, Doctor," murmured Sherry faintly, "but not quite in the way you expected." Her face was deathly white, and Fonseca caught her arm and guided her quickly to a chair.

"Mrs. Quinn, I don't understand. What is it you think has happened?"

"Those critters of yours, Doctor," Hutch answered for Sherry, who slumped in a chair.

"Yes?"

"They killed Sherry's little girl, and we think that poor fellow driving the truck as well."

"But that's nonsense! The flies were bred under the most rigorous of laboratory conditions."

"Mistakes have happened before," responded Hutch laconically.

"Even assuming that such a mutation occurred, it's simply inconceivable that they would kill humans."

"Well, you better start conceiving of it, Doctor, because it's the only thing that fits," interjected Sherry, at last regaining control.

"Fits what?" he demanded, a touch of belligerence in his voice.

"All the circumstances, the bizarre deaths," she snapped back. Quickly she outlined for him everything that she and Hutch had discovered. The condition of Pammy's body, the teenager in the truck, and finally Charles Edwards' description of the driver's body.

"Oh, my God," Fonseca whispered. With each new piece of information his skepticism weakened. The color had drained from his face, leaving him a sickly gray. "Donald," he whispered to his aide, "what have we done?"

Sherry had come prepared to hate this man, whom she believed to be the agent of Pamela's death, but in face of his terrible distress she could not sustain the anger.

Fonseca took both of her hands in his. "Mrs. Quinn, no words of apology can ever erase the harm that I've done to you, but accept them for whatever they're worth."

"Dr. Fonseca!" exclaimed his young assistant. "How do we even know that these people are telling the truth? They might be trying to drum up some sort of lawsuit so they can sue the government and collect a bundle."

Hutch's face darkened with fury, and he advanced on the slender scientist. "You're gonna eat those words, young fella." His voice was ominously low.

"Stop it! Both of you!" Sherry's voice cut, whip-like, through their anger.

"Yes, Mrs. Quinn is right, stop it!" Fonseca turned to his assistant. "I know it's not very 'scientific' Donald - call it a hunch - but I believe these people and I believe that our flies have become a menace. And even if they haven't, we have an obligation to investigate the situation. The question now," he continued, turning back to Sherry and Hutch, "is what do we do about it?"

"I hadn't gotten that far," Sherry admitted.

"I guess we ought to tell the authorities," Hutch suggested.

"Yes, the governor must be informed," agreed Fonseca.

"But will he believe us?" asked Sherry quietly.

"He has to," said the scientist grimly. "For if what we suspect is true, no one is safe. Every warm-blooded creature in the state is a potential host for the flies. Without action to stop the attacks, he could be governing a graveyard."

Chapter Seven

Philip Archuleta, governor of the state of New Mexico, stared morosely at the shelf of football trophies that hung on the wall opposite his desk. His law degree was hidden behind a tall plant to the left and behind his executive desk. Philip wasn't as proud of that, for he'd graduated at the bottom of his class, and it had taken him five tries to pass the bar. But football-now, that was another matter. He'd been the star quarterback for the University of New Mexico for three of the four years he'd attended.

Why couldn't life be like a football game? he thought wearily. But this time there was no one to throw the ball to. Federal cutbacks, energy-woes, water rights-he didn't know which way to turn, and he was afraid it was becoming obvious to the citizens of the state, and particularly to the press.

There was an urgent hammering on the door of the office. Archuleta frowned. His secretary, Hester, was usually much more discreet. From the sound of it, it had to be trouble. For a moment Archuleta considered pretending he wasn't in, then decided with a sigh that that was useless. After all, Hester had seen him arrive.

"Come in," he called reluctantly.

"Governor." The secretary's plump features were harried and her hair had tumbled from its prim bun. "There's a great crowd of people out here, and State Police Chief Wilson is here too. They all want to see *you*"

The governor winched at the unconscious and incredulous emphasis. "Who's this crowd, Hester?" he asked, stalling for time.

"A bunch of ranchers from up north. I can't get any sense out of them, and they're all quite hostile." Archuleta considered for a moment, then said, "Send in Chief Wilson."

"Yes, Governor."

Wilson entered almost immediately. His long narrow face was a melancholy mask, and his jaw clamped down hard on his cigar. "Philip, we got trouble," he announced without preamble.

"Oh, dammit, Frank, don't do that to me. I've just been on the phone with the state corrections department, and they're telling me there's likely to be another prison riot."

"Good," growled Wilson. "Let the bastards kill each other. Save the state some money. Besides I got *real* trouble for you."

He missed the governor's flinch, for he'd paused to light the thin cigar.

"One of my boys caught a couple of kids speeding on old Eighty-five. They were really moving too. Malcom clocked them at a hundred and ten. They gave him some story about how their town had been attacked by flies and everybody up there was dead. He figured they were high on something, so he hauled them in. They tested out clean, and they stuck to their story, so I decided to send somebody up to look." He paused to suck at the cigar.

"Well, what did they find?"

"Everybody in the whole damn town was dead."

"What?" Archuleta reared up from his chair, his mouth working as he gasped for air.

"Yep. It was really nauseating. I've been up there myself. In fact, I just got back."

"Which town?" Archuleta was pleased that his

voice had returned to its normal baritone range.

"Little burg called Moscón."

"No survivors?"

"Nope, just those two kids."

"What... what did they say killed the people?"

"Flies."

"Shit, man," moaned the governor, his head in his hands. "I can't deal with this. Maybe we could say it was plague. Sorry, stupid idea, forget that," he said, seeing the police chiefs expression. "Hey, maybe we could stick the feds. We could claim it was escaped nerve gas or something."

"Maybe we ought to be checking out what these kids said. If they're telling the truth, we could have a real crisis on our hands."

The governor lifted bloodshot eyes to Wilson. "But I'm running for that Senate seat."

The chief shrugged and started to speak, but the door burst open, and Hester was propelled into the room, gesticulating futilely at the thirty or so men who followed her.

"What in the hell-" exclaimed Archuleta, shrinking back in his chair.

"I'm sorry, Governor. I tried to stop them, but-"

"But we weren't being stopped," growled a big, powerfully built man whose belly lapped heavily over his beaten-silver belt buckle.

"Tell him, Bud."

"Yeah, give it to him."

"Tell him we ain't takin' anymore."

"Tell him we need help."

The voices rose on all sides a cacophony of anger and fear. The big man tossed his enormous cowboy hat onto a chair and advanced on the desk.

"My name is Bud Cliffton, you may have heard of me."

Archuleta gulped and nodded quickly. Every

politician knew of Bud Cliffton, owner of the largest ranch in New Mexico. Careers were sometimes broken on the rock of Cliffton's dislike.

"I got seven thousand head of cattle dead on my place, not to mention I don't know how many sheep and horses, and I lost one of my best hands, a good Indian kid." Cliffton's jaw worked as he struggled to control his anger and his grief. "All these men got similar stories to tell, and we want help. Now!"

"Do..." Archuleta cleared his throat and tried again. "Do you know what happened to your stock?"

"Be kind of hard to miss 'em when they come in, it's like a storm cloud rolling over you. Buzzin' and black and killin' everything in sight."

"Uh, flies, right?"

"That's right."

"How the hell did he know?"

"Why weren't we warned?"

"They knew all the time!"

The shouts battered at Archuleta. He gestured helplessly, trying to quiet the hubbub. Bud Cliffton swung around like a giant cruiser to face the other ranchers, and bellowed them down.

"That's enough!"

The silence was instantaneous.

"Now, back to our little problem, Governor. I sure would like to know how you knew about it and why you didn't see fit to tell any of us."

"I was just made aware of this terrible menace only moments before you came in." The politician's mask was back in place and the phrases fell glibly from his tongue. "Chief Wilson had just informed me of the tragic deaths in one of our small villages, a beautiful little place known as Malcan-"

"Moscón," corrected Wilson, unable to hide his contempt.

"Oh, oh, yes, of course, but as I was saying, now

that we know about the problem we will take immediate steps to solve it."

"Like what?" demanded several of the men.

"I'll contact the state agriculture department, and the pesticide control and inspection division, and we'll get right onto the matter."

"In other words, you're going to study the problem. Is that it, Governor?" Cliffton asked.

"We don't want to move ahead too precipitously and find ourselves in a worse mess."

"By the time your little commission finishes studying the problem, you will be in a bigger mess, Governor, and so will we - we'll all be dead!" The speaker was a skinny redhead who retreated back into the crowd, embarrassed by his outburst and the subsequent applause.

"Jessie's right," stated Cliffton. "We don't need talk or studies, we need action."

"I think the governor's well aware of that," broke in Wilson smoothly, "and I'm quite certain that the governor was about to suggest a spraying campaign."

"You're absolutely right, Frank. In light of this terrible crisis an immediate and massive spraying program is in order." He rose and extended his hand to Bud Cliffton. "I'm glad you came to see me about this matter, and let me assure you that action will be taken. Your families and your livestock will be protected." He threw Hester a speaking look, and she quickly herded the men from the office.

Archuleta frowned at one of his expensive woven Navajo rugs, which had been rumpled by the rancher's onslaught. Muttering, he hurried around the desk and twitched the rug back into place.

"Hadn't you better get started on that spraying?"

"Yeah. Jesus, Frank, this could cost the state a bundle! We've got the cost of the spraying, not to mention all the livestock killed. This could really hurt the economy!"

"People too," remarked the police chief ironically.

"Please, let me buy you lunch," said Robert Fonseca. "We won't say no," Hutch answered. "I don't know about Sherry, but I'm hungry. We left without eating this morning."

"I could use a drink," Sherry said with a wan smile. "In that case we'll go to the inn. The other two places in town worth eating at don't have liquor licenses."

Fonseca led them out a back door and into the employee parking lot. As Sherry sank into the unaccustomed comfort of the scientist's Cadillac El Dorado, she wearily reflected that even though she now knew what had killed Pammy, she was no closer to fulfilling her vow. The insects still had to be destroyed.

"Where are you from, Doc?" Hutch asked. "Massachusetts, originally - and call me Robert. I have a feeling we're going to be spending some time together."

"Because of the flies?" asked Sherry.

"Uh huh. You don't strike me as the kind of woman who can just go home and let the experts take over."

"No," she admitted softly. "I can't. They killed my child. I have to be a part of their destruction."

"Ah, the code of the West," murmured Fonseca.

"It's a pretty damn good code," Hutch responded belligerently, thinking that he sensed an easterner's condescension in Fonseca's words.

"Oh, absolutely, I couldn't agree more. Why do you think I want to stay in New Mexico rather than go back to the rat race on either coast."

"Sorry, I didn't mean to be so touchy."

"No problem."

A Dvorak piano quintet had been playing softly on the car radio. The piece ended, and a quiet-voiced announcer began the hourly newscast. Sherry, half-dozing in the air-conditioned comfort of the car, listened drowsily to the usual recitation of death, destruction, and alarm.

"On the local front, Governor Philip Archuleta today announced that a massive spraying operation will begin in northern New Mexico to combat an infestation of flies that are troubling farmers and ranchers in that part of the state."

"Listen!" Sherry ordered the two men who were deep into a sports discussion.

"No time has been set for the operation to begin, but sources in the Capitol indicate it could be as soon as the day after tomorrow."

"They're going to spray the flies!" Sherry said. Her eyes were bright with excitement and unshed tears. "It's over."

"But they mustn't!" Fonseca pulled agitatedly to the side of the road.

"Well, why the hell not?" demanded Hutch.

"I designed those flies to withstand most standard pesticides so that they could survive in California."

"So the poison won't do any good?" asked Sherry. "No, it's worse than that. The information that you've brought me indicates that the flies have mutated. It's possible - in fact, likely - that the spraying will lead only to further mutation. The insects could become even more deadly than they are now!"

"Oh, my God," Sherry murmured, her eyes wide with terror. "We've got to warn them, stop them." Fonseca swung the car back onto the road and pressed the pedal hard to the floor. "If we push it, we can be in Santa Fe in forty minutes. Then our only problem is getting in to see the governor."

"There goes lunch," Hutch muttered in an undertone. Sherry ignored him and directed her question to the scientist. "Doctor, do you think they'll listen to us?"

"I pray so, Sherry, but given the political mind, who knows?"

The trio peered cautiously into the outer office of the governor's wing, and at the implacable face of Hester C. de Baca.

"How are we gonna get past *that?*" Hutch whispered. "I've got an idea, just let me do the talking," Fonseca replied. Smoothing the coat of his elegant suit, the scientist gave his hair a quick comb and quickly shot Sherry and Hutch a thumbs-up sign. He walked boldly into the office with his hand outstretched.

"Hi," he called to the startled secretary. "I'm Bob Fonseca. I'm heading up a committee to elect Phil Archuleta, and I'd like to see the governor and present him with a check representing some of the money we've collected so far."

Flustered, Hester shuffled through the papers littering her desk. "I... I don't remember... any committee-"

"Newly started," he interrupted. "Now, can't we just have a minute of the governor's time?" He smiled. It was a particularly sweet and warm smile, and Sherry watched the middle-aged secretary blush beneath it.

"Well, I don't suppose it will do any harm." She disappeared through the inner door and emerged only moments later. "He'll see you now," she told Fonseca, and her eyes lingered on his stocky form as he led the other two into the office.

Archuleta stood behind his desk smiling what Sherry characterized as his Senate winning smile. "Mr. Fonseca, Bob, it's just great-"

"Governor, please forgive me, but I've practiced an unfortunate bit of duplicity in order to get in to see you."

"Oh?"

"My name is Dr. Robert Fonseca, but I'm not heading a committee for your Senate campaign. I'm a scientist at Los Alamos laboratories, and I'm the man who created those hell sent flies."

"What?"

"I genetically altered a particular strain of South American fly. It was my belief that they would prey upon the Mediterranean fruit flies currently plaguing California. The truck carrying the flies to the airport in Albuquerque overturned, and the flies were freed. I'm not certain what has caused the mutation, but the flies appear to be feeding on all warm-blooded creatures."

"So why come forward now?" Archuleta asked.

"It was only this morning that I learned of the mutation. These good people are apparently some of the first victims of the flies. Mrs. Quinn's daughter was killed by the creatures. But none of this is the reason for our visit. We heard on the radio that you are instituting a spraying program."

"That's right."

"Governor, you must not."

"Well, hell, I've got to do something. Those ranchers are on my neck!"

"I can appreciate that, sir, but I assure you that none of the standard chemical insecticides will stop these flies. They were bred to resist just such attacks. Further" - Fonseca held up a hand, forestalling Archuleta's next comment - "please, hear me out. I am utterly convinced that a spraying program will lead to further mutations. You've got to give me time to discover a way to stop the flies."

"Time is the one thing I don't have, Doctor. I've got to do something, and before the press gets a hold of this. Now, I'm a very busy man, so-"

"Please, you don't understand. If you spray and it leads to further mutations, we might *never* be able to destroy this menace!"

"Governor, listen to him!" Sherry cried. "You've never seen someone who's been killed by these insects. It's horrible." Tears began to flow down her cheeks. "If you act without knowing what will happen, you may kill hundreds-"

"Thousands," Fonseca amended.

Archuleta wavered. "How much time do you need, Doctor?"

"Three, four days. I'm sure I can have an answer by then."

"Four days! No way! If I don't act now, my ass is in the sling. I'm not blowing my chance for a Senate seat by waiting on some egghead to come up with an answer. I've talked to the people in the agriculture department, and they're certain this will work."

"But they don't know *these* flies," protested Fonseca. "Are you one hundred percent certain that spraying will cause these mutations?"

Fonseca hesitated, his innate scientific honesty forcing the answer. "No."

"Then I'm going ahead with the spraying. Now, if you don't get out of my office, I'm going to call the guards."

They stared, frustrated, at the governor. Hutch's hands clenched and unclenched at his sides, but finally with a disgusted snort he turned for the door. Sherry and Robert hesitated, but both seemed to realize that it was useless. Miserably they left.

"Well, maybe I'm wrong," Fonseca said once they stood on the sidewalk in front of the capitol.

"And if you're not?" demanded Hutch.

Robert shrugged helplessly. "Look, I'm going back to Los Alamos and see what I can do from that end. Research may be the only thing that's going to get us out of this. Do you want a ride back?"

Sherry considered, then shook her head. Even though the truck was still sitting in the parking lot of the labs, she couldn't face another drive.

"I'm too tired, Robert. If you could just drop us off at a hotel, we'll rent a car tomorrow and come back after the truck."

"Sure."

Hutch directed him to La Posada, an elegant old adobe near the plaza of downtown Santa Fe. The quiet comfort of the rooms was renowned and the cuisine was world-famous.

"Hutch, this is crazy," Sherry remonstrated with him as he guided her through the double doors into the lobby. "It's much too expensive."

"No counting pennies today," he said firmly. "We're both beat, and I'm not going to some fleabag hotel. If we're in for a fight, we may as well get prepared for it in the most comfortable surroundings possible."

She acquiesced, and soon they were in the room. It was decorated in the southwestern style, with a heavily carved double bed and a small corner fireplace. Sherry wished that it were winter and that she and Hutch were resting in this hotel just because they wanted to be together. She closed her eyes and imagined lying on the sheepskin rug before the fireplace while she and Hutch made languid love. With a sigh she relinquished the vision and dropped onto the bed. She began to tug at her boots, but Hutch dropped to one knee and carefully pulled them off.

He remained kneeling and watched as she pulled off her clothes. The sight of her slim body and high bosom made his mouth go dry, but the dark smudges beneath her eyes made him hurt for her, and he knew he wouldn't touch her. Sleep and rest were what she needed now, for he feared that before this had ended they would need all of their strength.

"Hold me, Hutch," she whispered.

He rose and quickly stripped. Lifting her, he pulled back the covers and gently deposited her in the bed. Her arms reached up to him, and he lay down beside her, nestling her head on his shoulder.

Her eyes closed, the sooty lashes quivering on her cheeks. He turned his head and pressed a gentle kiss onto her parted lips. Her arms tightened about him.

"Hutch, I'm scared."

"No need to be, darlin'," he said soothingly, but he thought, And so am I, darlin', so am I.

Chapter Eight

Sunset painted the western sky in bands of brilliant red, pink, and orange. In the canyon dusk had fallen, however, and a long line of headlighted cars wound up the highway to the entrance to the Santa Fe Opera. Uniformed police directed the cars across the highway and up this long climbing drive to the opera perched high on a mesa.

In the outer courtyard of the outdoor theater the operagoers milled about the two bars, or sat on rustic benches while they waited for the doors to open. Outfits ranged from faded Levi's and velvet blouses draped with masses of turquoise jewelry to designer gowns and tuxedos. Everyone carried a blanket or a long cloak, however, for even the summer nights were cold in the high desert.

Leslye Nenecker twitched her shawl irritably about her and searched the crowd for some sign of her husband. She'd sent him off minutes ago to get her a drink, and he still wasn't back. He was probably involved in some operatic or Old West discussion and had completely forgotten about her. Her mouth tightened into a thin line. She *needed* that drink! It was the only way she was going to survive the evening. God, how she hated opera and this wild country, and every year Howard dragged her from the comfort of New York to New Mexico for the Santa Fe season and an endless round of dude ranches.

The doors opened and a stream of people advanced on the four great portals manned by pretty girls in hand-woven serapes and black skirts who distributed programs and guided the attendees to their seats.

A small gray-haired man with wire-rim glasses bumped into Leslye, but he never paused in his single-minded drive toward the doors. The woman shot him a venomous look, but he seemed oblivious. His eyes were unnaturally bright, and he had the look of a religious fanatic on pilgrimage. He clutched his blanket closer to his stomach and pressed on through the crowd.

His name was Edgar Ptâcek, and he had traveled from Czechoslovakia for this night. To attend the opera in Santa Fe was a goal that had sustained him through all of the long gray years after 1969, and the Soviet invasion. For forty years he had played second cello in the Prague Philharmonic, and now he was dying.

A year ago the doctors had discovered the cancer that ate away at his stomach; then the need to leave, to reach America and the mountains north of Santa Fe had acquired an almost demented urgency. In desperation he had written to his cousin Illiana, and the money had been sent. A visa was next. It had taken five months, and finally it had been only the knowledge of his terminal illness that had convinced the authorities to release him. But now that was past. He was in Santa Fe for the opening night of the opera.

Once in the door he gazed up in awe at the great sweeping beams arching up toward the stars that glittered above his head. In the west the pinks and golds of the sunset still lingered, but over the opera night had fallen, a deep-blue mantle scattered with stars. Tears misted his eyes. Embarrassed, he removed his glasses and brushed his sleeve across his face. He found his seat and sat excitedly on the edge looking this way and that. The pain in his stomach gnawed at the edge of his consciousness, but it didn't matter. He could die tomorrow and it wouldn't matter. He had achieved his dream.

* * * * *

Giggling, the two young women hurried to the standing-room rail. In Albuquerque their dresses had seemed appropriate, but in the elegant surroundings of the opening-night crowd they were just what they seemed high-school prom gowns, carefully saved for an occasion such as this one.

"Do we look real silly?" Janice Keller whispered to her friend.

"No," responded Melissa McCloud with a chuckle. "Just semi-silly."

"Doesn't matter," Janice said, defiantly tossing her long black hair over one shoulder. "Pretty soon we're going to be up on that stage and all these people will be coming to hear us."

"I sure hope you're right. Somehow studying opera at the University of New Mexico doesn't sound too swift. Why did it have to be that awful Gary Tully who got to go to Rome to study?"

"No justice, that's all," stated Janice disgustedly. "Why can't we marry rich old men who would be content just to look at us and listen to us sing?"

"Make them brothers so we can all live together," suggested Melissa.

"*Twin* brothers," Janice embellished further.

"And they should be French," Melissa sighed. "English," Janice argued.

"French."

"English."

"Okay," Melissa said, surrendering. "They were separated at birth, and each raised in different countries."

"Done," Janice agreed, and they shook on it. "Actually, rich old men aside, I'd settle for Paolo Benzoni."

"No way," said Melissa. "He's mine."

"How come?"

"Because I'm a soprano, and you're a mezzo, and sopranos and tenors always end up together."

"So I get stuck with some hoary old bass while you get Mr. Gorgeous himself. I don't think that's very fair."

"No justice," Melissa said, sagely nodding her head.

They both laughed and, kicking off their high-heeled shoes, leaned comfortably on the padded rail.

Paolo Benzoni sat quietly in his dressing room. Gently he touched the dazzling headdress that he would wear as Tamino in Act I of *Magic Flute.* He had sung the role twelve or thirteen times, but this time was different. This was Santa Fe, where the music of the wind and the songs of the insects blended harmoniously with the orchestra.

In the hall outside his room he could hear the happy chatter of the apprentices as they prepared for their first performance. It was a good system and he wished that other opera houses would adopt it.

The director of the Santa Fe Opera combed the finest music schools in America and Europe for young singers. These young people, all aspiring soloists, provided the chorus for the operas. In return they were allowed to understudy the major roles and take classes provided by the opera.

Yes, it was a good plan, and there was one young apprentice who had drawn him. She was a tiny coloratura with deep green eyes and bright, bouncing red curls. She was singing Papagena tonight, and he envied Max, who got to hold and cuddle her.

Benzoni smiled at his image in the mirror. His

teeth were very white against the dark of his beard and mustache. Tonight there would be a party at the ranch house, and who could tell, perhaps the delightful little soprano would spend the evening in his bed. He hoped so. His eyes narrowed, giving him a rakish, piratical look.

There was a discreet knock on the door.

"Time, sir," called the stage manager.

"I come," he called picking up the elaborate headdress. Opening the door, he stepped into the hall and made his way swiftly to the wings. The backstage was cluttered with sets, props, and actors. He dodged the fifty-foot dragon that would pursue him onto the stage at the beginning of the opera. At last he reached his position. The only things left now were the waiting and the nerves. He closed his eyes, preparing to sing.

The conductor stepped through the small door at the rear of the orchestra pit and walked swiftly to the podium. A ground swell of applause followed his entrance. He briefly acknowledged the audience with a regal inclination of his silver head. Turning, he raised his baton. A hush of anticipation swept the house. The slender stick fell, and the great opening chords of the overture filled the air.

The sound rose, soaring into the desert night. And from behind the juniper and piñon dotted hills the flies rose too. A buzzing black curtain blotted the view of the mountains beyond the stage. A moan of dismay swept the audience, and the music was drowned out beneath the beating of the hideous wings.

The flies struck in great clotted masses that settled onto the vulnerable flesh trapped beneath them. Screams and curses filled the air as people fought to free themselves from the confines of their seats. Janice and Melissa screamed with pain as the stinging insects descended. Blindly they raced for the door. Melissa, smaller and lighter, slipped through into the false safety of the outer courtyard, but the flies waited there too.

Janice struggled with her long skirt. She reached the door, but her foot slipped on the satin hem of her dress and she went down in a tangle of petticoats and blanket. She fought to rise, but the crowd had reached her. Panicked, driven only by the need to survive, they trampled her beneath their running feet. She shrieked in agony as a spiked heel drove completely through her outstretched hand. The pounding agony continued, but soon she was oblivious. Her pretty pink dress was slowly stained an ugly clashing red.

When the flies attacked, Edgar didn't fight to escape as did the people around him. Death was an old companion. Instead, he wept with misery and frustration. Not tonight, nor ever again, would there be the music. Suddenly he shook a fist skyward and began to climb laboriously over the seats.

The rows were filled with twisted bodies, but he ignored the carnage about him, and the bites of the flies, and pressed on. At last he reached the lip of the orchestra pit. The flies ate at him even as he fell into the pit.

Lifting blood-blind eyes, he saw his prize. The cello had fallen to the floor, its rich brown surface smeared with the blood of its owner. Edgar dragged himself to the instrument. Tenderly he enfolded it in his arms. Now it was time to die.

Howard Nenecker was no fool. When he saw the nightmare descend, he knew there was no escape. Leslye had screamed over and over, her face a twisted mask of hysteria, but he hadn't released her. Reaching beneath his jacket, he pulled out the small .45 he had purchased for protection.

Murmuring endearments, he placed it firmly against the base of her skull and fired. Grinning savagely, he thrust the gun into his mouth.

Just like the pioneers, came the insane little thought. They would kill their women and children to keep them from falling into the hands of the marauding Indians. He should have fought back, he thought with a moment of sadness.

No use, he decided, and he resolutely pulled the trigger.

It took a few minutes for the flies to decipher the maze of the backstage. Many of the singers had rushed onto the stage when the screams had begun, though some of the musicians in the orchestra continued to play, trying to ignore the commotion and still unaware of its deadly cause.

Benzoni, who had been a child during the war, had learned caution in his mother's milk. He peered around one wing and watched with horror as the flies descended in clouds upon the helpless singers on the stage.

He suddenly frowned, puzzled as a clot of flies ignored a tall young man who seemed frozen with fear, and instead plowed into a massive piece of scenery. They struck with such force that they left an oozing trail on the painted flat. Many of the flies were behaving in a bizarre fashion: flying aimlessly up and down, spiraling into the floor, careening into scenery. Then, as the last discordant notes from the orchestra died, the insects seemed to right themselves. Infused with purpose once more, they continued their bloody feast.

Benzoni pulled back, feeling his dinner fighting its way up to choke him. Regaining control, he quickly scanned the backstage. A few singers and stagehands remained. With them was the tiny redhead. He felt a stab of joy that she had not become one of those faceless horrors on the stage. The question now was how to keep her from so becoming one... and himself with her? His mind cast frantically about for some means of escape.

Her eyes met his, and she came to his side as if knowing he would protect her. But how? How? his mind screamed silently. The buzzing filled his ears, making it hard to think. A lazy summer afternoon filled with the angry drone of bees, and he a boy of nine or ten hiding in the pond to escape their ire after he had robbed them of their honey.

Gripping the girl's hand, he shouted to the milling people.

"Come, come quickly before you die."

A few followed, but most continued to run heedlessly in all directions. His jaw tightened, but there was nothing he could do to help them. If he delayed now, all would die. Gesturing quickly, he brought his few people into a close circle with him.

"We have very little time." Stress had made his accent very thick. "Directly behind the stage is a deep canyon. Through it flows a stream that should be deep enough to protect us. Stay under the water and come up only enough to take a quick breath. Then if the Virgin is kind, we all may survive this night. Now come."

The small group rushed to the edge of the stage in back. It was a dangerous position, for now they were revealed to the flies. Paolo and one of the stagehands worked frantically to lower the others to the ground. The singer glanced over his shoulder and saw the swarm coming. He released the hands of the young woman whom he supported, and swung over the precipice. Taking a deep breath, he dropped even as the flies settled onto his hands, biting and stinging.

He sprinted for the stream, feeling the bites of the leading insects. His breath came in great gasps, and he decided that he was much too old and fat for such activities. The canyon loomed up before him. He pushed forward with a last burst and plunged into the water twenty feet below. The stream was fairly shallow, and his body was bruised and cut by the sharp rocks hidden beneath the water. Benzoni drew a deep breath and sank beneath the gurgling water. He welcomed the pain of the stones and his bruises, for he was still alive.

The flies continued their ghastly feast. When the living had been dealt with, the insects turned their attention to the dead, those trampled and smothered by the crowd. This blood was not as fresh, but it satisfied the creatures' frenzied hunger.

The last faint rays of the sun vanished from the west and night wrapped the mountains. And the flies, replete, departed. The beautiful theater was a mass of twisted bodies. The concrete aisles ran with gore and blood dripped from the seats.

Hours later Benzoni joined the few survivors who emerged wet and shivering, from the stream. They crept back up the mountain to the theater. Stunned by the carnage, they fled back to Santa Fe.

The opera had become a playhouse for the dead.

Chapter Nine

"Think we ought to be heading back to the ranch?" The sunlight streaming through the windows of the restaurant turned Sherry's hair to silver. Her eyes flew to Hutch's face, and in them he read fear.

"I... I guess."

"Sherry, honey, what is it?"

She hesitated, spinning her coffee cup in its saucer. The dark liquid sloshed over the rim and spattered onto the white tablecloth. Nervously she mopped at the stain with her napkin, still not answering. "Sherry?" he prompted again.

"I don't know, Hutch. I feel like maybe we ought to stay close to the center of things, and yet I know, if I'm honest with myself, that that's not the sole reason." She paused and gazed out at the deceptively peaceful courtyard of the hotel. "I'm scared." The tone was so low that Hutch had to lean forward to hear her.

"Of them flies, honey?"

She nodded, a quick agitated little movement. "If they came after us up at the ranch, there's nothing we could do. Nothing."

"But those poor dumb beasts are up there, and they'd have to face those bugs all alone. It just goes against my grain to leave them defenseless."

"But we're just dumb beasts too, and we'll die just as horribly as those cattle."

"Easy now, honey," murmured Hutch,

uncomfortably aware of the curious looks from the other diners. She threw down her napkin and turned again to the window. Her teeth worried her lower lip, and Hutch could see that she was struggling not to cry.

"Okay, darlin', well stay. Now finish your breakfast."

"I'm not hungry."

"You want to go?"

She nodded, shoved back her chair, and hurried from the restaurant, leaving Hutch to pay. Waiting in the lobby, she paced out the pattern on the black and red Navajo rug.

"Excuse me."

Startled, she turned to face the desk clerk. "Yes?"

"Are you Sherry Quinn?"

"Yes, I am."

"Telephone call for you," he said, extending the receiver. Before she reached the desk, he pulled back the phone, saying, "By the way, your description was perfect, mister."

She accepted the receiver, wondering who could have traced her to La Posada.

"This is Fonseca."

"Oh, good morning-"

"No time to talk! Get yourself to a television."

"What? Why?" But the phone was dead.

"Is there a television in the lobby?" she demanded of the young man behind the desk.

"No, but there's one in the manager's office."

"Please, can I use it? This will take only a moment."

"Sure."

Hutch, shoving his wallet into his hip pocket, strolled into the lobby. Sherry grabbed his hand and pulled him after the clerk.

"What's goin' on?"

"Fonseca called and said there was something on

TV that we had to see."

"Good, he's out," whispered the clerk as he entered the cramped office. The boy snapped on the television and hurried back to his post. The picture came up, revealing Big Bird.

"That can't be it," muttered Hutch. He flipped channels until he found what seemed to be a special newscast. A ferret faced woman, whom Hutch recognized as an Albuquerque reporter, was holding a microphone before a large bearded man. There was a long scrape across his forehead and he looked exhausted. He spoke with a heavy Italian accent.

"...killed everyone."

"Signor Benzoni, it's an absolute miracle that you survived."

"No miracle," he said firmly. "I was given enough time to think, and I acted upon it. I remembered that insects do not like water, and I knew that the stream was flowing below the opera. I wish I could have helped more people, but they were mad with fear."

"What happened?" cried Sherry, pounding her fists on the uncommunicative screen.

The unctuous newscaster turned back to face the camera. "And there you have it, ladies and gentlemen. Last night tragedy struck at the Santa Fe Opera. According to the few survivors, one of whom is Signor Paolo Benzoni, the famous Italian tenor, the opera was attacked by hordes of flies. Well, whatever the cause of the holocaust, the fact remains that over two thousand people lie dead this morning."

"They don't believe him," Sherry said. "Why won't the governor admit what's happening so that people can be prepared?"

"I don't know, baby."

They flipped to another channel where a small redhaired girl was being interviewed. "I couldn't see very much," she said softly, "but I was close enough to the stage to be able to see part of the audience if I leaned forward. I think what was so horrifying was that the insects seemed to be intelligent. It's as if they knew that the people in the theater were trapped. The way they appeared when everyone was in their seats and the overture had begun - it was eerie."

The show cut into a commercial for a popular breakfast cereal. Hutch leaned over and flipped off the television. Sherry sat silently with her arms wrapped about her slender body.

"Hutch," she whispered. "What if they are intelligent? They could kill us all."

"Sherry, now that's just plain silly! They're just bugs. Maybe a little tougher than the kind we're used to, but still just bugs."

"But nobody's doing anything."

"Dr. Fonseca is, and the state's going to spray."

"And what if Robert is right? What if the spray doesn't even hurt them, but only makes them worse?" Wordlessly he slipped his arms about her rigid body. She clung to him as if his warmth and life could sustain her.

"Hutch, they must be intelligent. They haven't spread out across the countryside the way normal flies would have. They're staying together and hunting in a pack."

"That's true," he said slowly.

She pulled from his arms and began to pace the room. "If they hunt together this way, they must all be staying together. There's got to be a central lair, a nest where they're striking from."

"It sure would help the doc if we could find that nest. If it exists, that is."

"I'm sure it exists, and you're right. It would be easier for Robert to destroy them if we could catch them all in one place."

"You want to go lookin'?"

She hung her head, considering. "No, not until

after the spraying. Who knows, maybe it will kill them."

"Yeah, no sense us putting our asses on the line if the insecticide is going to do it for us."

"Then we wait. And, oh, God, Hutch, I hope we're right for delaying."

Dennis "Buckey" Adams paused and spat. The stream of brown fluid splattered accurately against the wheel of his plane. He grinned and shifted the wad of tobacco to the other cheek. Being called up for extra duty didn't bother Buckey. He'd been a member of the air national guard for seven years, and he loved the weekends spent playing soldier. The current assignment wasn't all that great, spraying flies up north, but he could pretend they were gooks, and that would pass the time.

He climbed into the cockpit of his A7 and waited for the tower to okay his takeoff. Idly he wondered why the governor had called in the national guard for this operation instead of some commercial sprayers. Still, it didn't do to question orders: just carry them out. The okay came and he lifted into the cloudless blue sky, heading north. With him flew seven other planes, all loaded with malathion.

On one long sweeping run Buckey noticed a herd of animals running panicked across the flat grasslands of Colfax County. Frowning, he banked and brought the plane in low for a closer look. A cloud of darkness pursued the fleeting cattle.

Here at last was the enemy. For the past two hours all he'd done was spray the placid countryside, but here was the real thing. He increased the throttle until he flew directly over the mass of flies. Grinning savagely, he punched the button, releasing his cargo of poison directly onto the creatures, who had already begun to feed upon the stragglers of the herd.

The veil of mist settled onto the seething bodies. Buckey banked once more and came in for another look.

He wanted to watch his victims die, the way he had never been permitted to during the war. His grin of pleasure faded, for the flies were continuing their assault. Furiously he released another burst of insecticide. The result was the same - nothing.

His hand shot out, reaching for the radio, then froze. HQ was always tough on a commander who reported failure. His plump face twisted with indecision. On the other hand, he thought, HQ needed complete information. He figured that those other bozos probably hadn't tried a close-in run the way he had. They wouldn't know if the spray was working or not. Therefore, the man who could keep HQ accurately informed would probably come out smelling like roses.

He wiped away the sweat that had beaded his upper lip, and flipped on the radio. God, it felt good to have made a decision.

The emergency room stank of blood, pus, sweat, and fear. Kathy Littlebird cautiously pulled open the street door and slipped into the melee. She glanced quickly about the crowded room, but there were no police in sight. McNee had tipped her off about the sudden deluge of patients into the emergency room of St. Francis' Hospital.

The day of the spraying she had gone to the capitol and spent the morning lurking about the governor's office in the hopes of hearing how the operation was going. What she had heard was exactly nothing, but the way aides kept rushing in and out of Archuleta's office indicated that something was up. She had just returned to the *Courier's* offices, hot and frustrated, when McNee's call had come.

He'd sounded like a man who'd been through hell and was still living in some vestige of the nightmare.

"I've been at it since early this morning," he'd told her. "It's like something out of Dante up there. Whole villages filled with stripped bodies, and I keep passing wrecked cars on the highway. They're all faceless, and... and their windows are always open. I'm terrified to get out of the unit when we do find someone still alive. I'm convinced they're going to be onto me next. It's like the creatures have gone mad! They attack anything warm-blooded. No one is safe!" His voice rose hysterically. Kathy realized that if she were going to get anything useful out of him, she'd have to snap him out of it, and quickly.

"Okay, Devon, but why call me?" Her flat uninterested tone brought him up short.

"Un... uh... well, I think they're trying to cover this up."

"That's crazy!" Kathy exploded, shaken out of her act. "With people dying everywhere, how in the hell do they think they can keep it quiet?"

"I don't know, but I sure think they're trying. There are police stationed in the emergency rooms of every hospital from here to the Colorado border."

"And how do you know that?"

"I checked with some of my friends who drive the far north circuit."

"Can you get me into St. Francis'?" she demanded.

"Sure, if you're willing to dress as a rescue worker."

"Honey, I'd dress as Santa Claus to get a lead on this."

And now she was there. She pulled her white jacket tighter about herself, hiding the camera. She peered over the shoulder of one doctor and, nauseated, decided that maybe she wouldn't use the camera. She didn't know if she could deal with developing the picture.

Half of the man's face was gone. Bone shone white through the tatters of scarlet flesh. Two beds over, a woman screamed, a tearing, spiraling sound that made the journalist long to cover her ears. Littlebird forced herself to turn and look at the horror on the bed.

The woman's nude body was a mass of sores, and each one was seething, writhing, exploding open in putrid fountains of pus, flesh, and larvae. Gleaming wetly, their obscene worm bodies oozed from the woman's body. The scream reached a peak beyond human endurance and cut off. Her bulging eyes rolled back into her skull. Silently the nurse at her side pressed shut the lids over the staring eyes. Kathy felt the bile rising, but she fought it back. To lose control now would expose her, and someone had to penetrate the shroud of secrecy the authorities had thrown about the crisis.

Quietly, unobtrusively she toured the ward, noting the bloody flesh of those who had served to feed the flies' seemingly insatiable need for blood, the raving deaths of those who had been the repositories for the flies' eggs, and the helpless almost shell-shocked expressions on the faces of the doctors and nurses who struggled against the ever-increasing odds.

At last she could stand it no longer. She slipped once more into the parking lot where McNee waited by his ambulance. As she entered, she ducked her head and glanced fearfully skyward.

"Sort of gets to you, doesn't it?" McNee asked softly.

"No shit," she muttered.

"Tell me, Kathy, do you think this is the end of the world?"

She raised her head, tossing back her dark curls, but the flip answer died in her throat as the sights in the emergency room washed over her once more.

"Maybe it is, Devon. And may God have mercy on us, because I don't think the flies will."

Chapter Ten

"Governor! Please, you've got to reconsider!" The young aide's scrubbed, all-American face was tight with concern. The tails of his Brooks Brothers' suit flapped as he rushed to keep pace with the governor's long-legged strides.

"Absolutely not!" Archuleta said, making a slashing gesture through the air with one hand. "If we cancel the government workers' picnic, the press will *know* that something's up. So far we've managed to keep them at bay. And we've got to keep them away, at least until we can figure out what to do since the spraying failed."

"But, sir, what if they attack the picnic?"

The politician seemed to blanch at the thought, then he straightened his shoulders and thrust out his chin stubbornly. "They were last sighted up around Dulcy. Also, aside from that thing with the Santa Fe Opera, they've avoided the large population centers. I really don't think there's any danger."

"B-but, sir," stammered the aide, looking like he wanted to cry. "The picnic isn't in a large population area. It's up in the Pecos wilderness, miles from anything."

Archuleta whirled on the younger man. With his face only inches from the aide's, he spat, "Look, asshole, this is an election year. Do you want that job in Washington? Then keep your mouth shut, because if anything happens to my campaign *I* won't make it to the Senate and *you* won't make it to Washington! You got that?"

The man's Adam's apple bobbed frantically above the stiff white collar. He hesitated, staring into Archuleta's furious brown eyes, then he abruptly nodded.

"Good! Now I'm taking my wife and kids up to that picnic. I should be back in about two hours, and we'll get back on this fly mess."

"Yes, sir."

Damn incompetent fools, he thought as he hurried through the marble halls of the capitol. These young hotshots just didn't know how the game was played. This was politics, after all. He shoved open the heavy glass doors and stepped into the parking lot. He quickly scanned the cars until he spotted his bronze Cadillac. María was waiting, already seated on the passenger side. She waved when she saw him. Through the glass of the back window he could see Tomás and Bonita bouncing up and down on the seat.

He crossed the expanse of asphalt. It was already shimmering from the heat even though it was only nine o'clock. He pulled open the door and slid in next to his wife.

Her long black hair was coiled expertly on her head, making her slender white neck seem even longer and more fragile than usual. As he gazed at her ebon and ivory loveliness, Archuleta wondered with a shudder if he were making a mistake. Then the vision of her overseeing an elegant brownstone in Washington, D.C., made him push the disquieting thought aside. He had to give her a setting worthy of her, and somehow he had to be worthy of her himself.

Everyone had wondered how Philip Archuleta, son of a mechanic and a waitress in Albuquerque, had married María Ramona Josefa Ramírez. She was the child of one of New Mexico's most powerful northern Spanish families, and she had been bred to wealth and power. They had met at the university and soon had decided to marry. Her family had fought the match bitterly, but María had proved that she was as tough as Doha Ramona, the powerful matriarch of the Ramírez clan. She had married Philip, and even old Ramona had danced at their wedding.

Archuleta had entered politics as a way to power and wealth. He was determined to shed his lower-class Albuquerque connections and at last be accepted by María's aristocratic family, but beyond this, he wanted María happy and he wanted to give her everything.

He leaned over and pressed a gentle kiss onto her softly curving lips.

"Me too, Daddy," clamored Bonita, his five-year-old daughter. She was standing on the backseat, her plump arms outstretched to hug him. Her Levi's coveralls had a white cat embroidered on the bib. She paused to pat the yarn cat before once more lifting her face for his kiss. He inched around between the steering wheel and the seat and hugged her, breathing deeply of her child smell.

Tomás watched with eight-year-old indulgence while Bonita received her embrace. When Archuleta set the little girl back on the seat, he turned to face his son. Tomás gave him a gap-toothed grin and threw a mock punch at his father. Laughing, Philip leaned over the seat and tickled the little boy, who shrieked with laughter.

"We'd better hurry," María reminded him softly. "The people like to know that even if the governor can't be with them, his family will be."

He nodded and put the sleek car into gear. They headed north out of Santa Fe and into the Sangre de Cristo Mountains. As they climbed higher into the pine-scented forests, the heat eased, and among the sighing pines Archuleta felt himself begin to relax for the first time in days.

A large hand-painted cardboard sign shouted out STATE PICNIC, and a red arrow pointed down a narrow dirt road. The governor spun the wheel and jounced down the rutted road to the picnic area. A large crowd had already gathered, and were busy setting up for the festivities. Women unpacked cases of hot dog and hamburger buns, relishes, meats, and drinks, while the men strung volleyball nets and started fires in the blackened barbecue pits.

People shouted greetings as Archuleta pulled up. He crossed to the passenger side and helped María from the car; then, slipping an arm around her slender waist, he smiled and waved at the assembled crowd. He turned back to the car and, opening the back door, lifted out his daughter. Tomás scorned such help and leaped happily to the ground.

"I wish you could stay," María whispered against his ear.

"So do I, but there's a problem that just won't wait. I'll be back for you at three, and if I can't make it, I'll send Max." He pressed another kiss on her mouth. She drew back, faintly surprised by his ardor, for such demonstrations in public weren't part of their life.

"Sorry," he said. "I just don't want to leave you."

"There's nothing wrong, is there?" A slight frown marred the smooth beauty of her oval face.

A sudden constriction squeezed his chest, but he forced himself to smile. "No, of course not, darling. You and the kids have a good time and think of me slaving back in the city."

"I save a hot dog for you, Daddy," lisped Bonita, tugging at his coat.

"You do that, sweetie, and I'll eat it when we drive back home."

He kissed the children one last time and climbed back into the Cadillac.

María Ramona Josefa Ramírez watched the car vanish in a cloud of dust kicked up by the rapidly spinning wheels, and felt sadness. She knew that in many ways he was a small man in a very, very big job, but it didn't matter. She loved him, and was proud and happy to be his wife.

"The food will be ready in a little while," she said to her children. "So, what would you like to do now?"

"I want to go down to the stream," bawled Tomás.

"Wanna drink," added Bonita.

"Okay, you go on down to the stream, but be careful and don't get wet all over."

"Ah, Mom..."

"I mean it," she admonished, one expensively manicured finger held up warningly.

"Okay," he muttered. He scuffed away for a few steps, then broke into a run.

"Now your drink, honey," the woman said, taking her daughter by the hand. "What do you want?"

"Coke."

"Oh, those cavities," María murmured to herself, and joined a group of women clustered about a large cooler.

María obtained a Coke for her beaming daughter and helped the other women set out paper plates and plastic utensils. Through the trees she could just see Tomás splashing happily in the swiftly flowing stream with a group of boys. His new cowboy boots tilted drunkenly against each other on the edge of the stream. She smiled fondly, thinking how much he looked like Philip.

Hamburgers and hot dogs began to roast over the open fires. The smell of their sizzling juices mingled with the tangy scent of pine and juniper. Once the sandwiches were ready, they were placed between buns and left on a large platter for the hungry picnickers to grab as they pleased.

María had turned to help a little boy open a jar of relish. Behind her, Bonita crept to the loaded platter and snatched a hot dog from the pile. Glancing hastily at her mother, the child stuffed the sandwich down the front pocket in the bib of her coveralls.

The afternoon advanced, and María dozed against a large tree stump. Tomás had gobbled a hamburger and returned to his games in the stream.

The sound, when it came, blended pleasantly with the murmur of the wind in the trees and the gurgle of the water. The woman never even opened her eyes.

An agonizing stinging clawed through her cheek, and with a cry María leaped to her feet, slapping at the insect. Her slim, beringed hand smashed several of the vermin, but thousands followed. With a moaning gasp she slid back down the dead and twisted tree. The flies crawled hungrily through her elaborate coiffure.

The screams of the dying ripped through the dreamy stillness of the mountains. Tomás threw aside the stick with which he'd been doing battle with wicked monsters, and climbed from the stream. He slipped on the moss-slimed rocks and fell headlong into the water, cutting his head on an outcropping rock. Blood ran into his eyes, and he began to snivel for his mother. When she didn't come, he drew his sleeve across his nose and ran back to the picnic area searching for her. Stones and brambles cut at his bare feet. Branches whipped into his face, and he began to cry from the pain. Suddenly the hurt was magnified beyond all endurance as he ran headlong into a cloud of the raging insects. They settled onto his face and feet, eating their way inward toward the soft body tissues that sustained them.

Bonita stood with her dimpled hands wrapped about a fat hot dog as people staggered past her. Her dirty face was streamed with tears of fear, for the screams of the dying terrified her. She remained rooted in place, wailing pitifully for her parents, but only the flies came. Her soft brown eyes widened with the child's incomprehension of hurt and pain. Soon only the gaping sockets stared blindly at the sky.

Slowly the flies lifted from the chewed bodies of their victims. Bloated, almost lethargic after their feast, they rose into the afternoon sky, blotting the sun, and vanished into the north.

Nothing had been settled in the five-hour meeting. The governor, his aides, and the commander of the air national guard were no closer to a solution for the fly crisis than before. To Archuleta's weary brain it seemed that the possible solutions hung rejected in the smoky air of his office. Try another spraying; call in the feds; do nothing; call in the scientists at Los Alamos and Sandia...

He looked at his watch with relief and, rising, announced that he had to pick up his wife and children. He had not managed to escape, however, for several of his aides piled into the car with him, and the discussion had continued all the way into the Pecos.

Their voices ground on him, and gritting his teeth, he ignored them, concentrating instead on the twisting curves of the high mountain road. He almost missed the turnoff, for the cardboard sign had fallen over and lay half-hidden in the weeds. Slamming on the brakes, he spun the wheel and careened onto the side road.

As they jounced down the rutted track, a growing terror began to gnaw at the lining of his stomach. There was no noise. Only the flutter of the laboring air-conditioner and the mutterings of his aides broke the brooding silence that held the forest. He jammed the accelerator to the floor as dread warred with certainty.

Lewis Dobson, his chief adviser, gave a shout of warning, but it was too late. Archuleta frantically fought the wheel, but the car jerked and bounced as the right front tire crunched sickeningly over a body.

"Oh, God," whimpered Bruce Pearson, his baby-blue eyes moist with terror. "You've killed him! What are we gonna do? We'll never win now!" Hysteria whined in his voice.

"Shut up," spat Dobson, smashing Pearson across the mouth with the back of his hand. "He was dead already." Pearson subsided, staring at the ex-Vietnam officer with dread.

Archuleta brought the car to a lurching stop and leaped from the vehicle. His face was a grimacing mask as he ran through the bloated bodies searching for his family.

Suddenly he skidded to a halt and fell to his knees in the dust. An embroidered white kitten stared mischievously up at him. Trembling, he pulled the limp form into his arms and held it tightly against his chest. Blood smeared the gray of his suit. He felt the bulge in the pocket of the coveralls. Slowly, with infinite care, he withdrew the hot dog, and the cry that was torn from his throat resembled nothing human.

"Martínez," snapped Dobson. The young Spanish lawyer wiped the vomit from his lips and shakily turned to face his superior. "Get down to the ranger station and radio for help." Dobson walked to where Archuleta squatted in the dust. He never looked to see if Martínez had obeyed-it was assumed.

He removed the torn carcass from the governor's arms and pulled him to his feet. Archuleta's sobs ripped through the silence, affecting even Dobson.

"Phil," he said softly. "We've got to look around. Maybe María or Tomás managed to escape." Archuleta knuckled his eyes and drew a shaky breath. Dobson kept a hand beneath the governor's elbow, supporting and guiding him, and they hunted through the grisly mounds.

Soon they had located Tomás and María. Archuleta collapsed like a mannequin whose strings had been cut. He stared stupidly from shock-darkened eyes.

"Phil, we've got to have help." There was no response. "You've got to call in the federal government," There was still nothing. With a sigh Dobson turned back to gaze at the devastation before him. He dug his hands deep into the pockets of his pants and debated.

With a few stiff drinks he knew he could get Archuleta articulate once more. They would then call Washington, and after that it wouldn't matter if the governor were a zombie. Dobson knew he could handle things.

"We've got to stop them." The voice was rusty. It seemed to grind from Archuleta's throat. "No matter what it takes, Lewis, we've got to stop them."

Lewis Dobson pushed over a body with the toe of his expensive shoe. Thoughtfully he considered that it might take more than the governor was willing to pay to stop the menace. But that didn't matter. In a fight for survival sometimes sacrifices had to be made. If Philip Archuleta didn't have the stomach for them... The ex-Marine smiled mirthlessly. Well, he, Lewis Dobson, did.

Chapter Eleven

The pile of books crashed down on the scarred surface of the desk. Sherry jumped and Fonseca looked contrite.

"Sorry, it was a bit of a load."

"I'll say," muttered Hutch, sorting through the books. *"The Habits of the Fly "* he read, and shook his head.

"Robert, couldn't you just summarize these. We really don't have time to become experts on flies."

"You're right. I don't know what possessed me to bring all this in. I guess I'm too used to working with graduate students. You want coffee before we launch into it?"

"Please," Sherry answered fervently. She and Hutch had ridden the bus up from Santa Fe early that morning to collect the pickup and see what Fonseca had found. The truck was intact, but the scientist had had little luck in isolating a way to destroy the flies.

"Why do you want a lecture?" asked Robert, returning with three precariously balanced cups.

"Hutch and I were wondering if it were possible for the flies to have some central nesting place. If so, and if we could find it, we thought it would help you when the time came to move against them."

"Even though flies don't normally live in colonies, I won't discount the idea. None of the norms seem to apply where these beasts are concerned." Fonseca sighed deeply, running a hand wearily over his face. "Ah, yes, where to begin? Flies primarily live in filth."

"Great," Hutch mumbled, blowing on his coffee.

"Standard breeding places are in manure or garbage, so a stockyard or a dump would be definite possibilities for your nest."

"One problem with that," Sherry offered. "People would have noticed if the flies were inhabiting a dump or a stockyard."

"Only if it were a known site," Hutch said. "There are a lot of little ghost towns in the north country. They all had their garbage dumps and I doubt any of them were covered."

"Good point," Sherry mused.

"But what a frightful undertaking," Fonseca objected. "You could spend weeks in such a search and still come up with nothing. You would also be placing yourselves directly in the flies' territory." His eyes devoured Sherry's delicate face and Hutch felt a stab of jealousy. "No, I can't permit you to take such a risk."

"But what other choice do we have?" The chair was thrust back with an ear-splitting screech, and Sherry began to pace agitatedly about the lab. "There are people living up there who can't hide in Santa Fe or Albuquerque. So how could I do that? I vowed I was going to destroy whatever killed my daughter. Am I supposed to back down now just because it looks tougher or more dangerous than first expected? No, I've got to see it through, even if it means combing the north country for the rest of my life."

The two men gazed at her flushed, impassioned face. Abashed, they dropped their eyes to their rapidly cooling coffee.

"Okay, honey," Hutch said finally. "I'm with you." Wordlessly she crossed to him and wrapped her arms about his neck. Fonseca stared intently at the far wall and tried not to care or to worry. It was evident that nothing he could say would dissuade this remarkable woman from her course.

"When will you start out?" he asked heavily.

"Not for a couple of days. I don't want to have to keep coming back to Santa Fe or Española to sleep, so we'll have to stock up on supplies."

"You're going to camp out up there?" cried Fonseca.

"It'll save us time, Robert. I don't see that we have a choice."

"All right," he agreed again. "And I'll keep working on this end so that your work won't be for nothing."

Sherry smiled warmly and took his hands. "It sounds like a good deal to me. Now, Hutch and I will get out of here and let you get back to work."

The door closed behind the departing couple, but for a long while the scientist didn't return to his experiments. Instead he stared at his hands, reliving the touch and feel of Sherry Quinn.

Hutch pulled the pickup to the side of the rutted dirt road and parked beneath an enormous pine tree. Dust hung in the lower branches and not even an insect chorus disturbed the brooding heat.

Sweeping off his hat, the man wiped his arm across his forehead, removing sweat and further tangling his matted hair. With a sigh he picked up a yellowing map and peered at the spiderweb of lines. Sherry sat silently next to him, head thrown back against the seat, eyes tightly closed.

"We look to be some eight or nine miles from Fargo. You want to go on or you want to camp for the night?"

With a sigh that was almost a groan the woman pushed herself upright. After three days in the truck her bottom was beginning to strongly object to the feel of the vinyl seat.

"How much daylight left?"

"Two, three hours."

"Then let's go on." She settled back into her position. Hutch stared at her, opened his mouth to argue, then shut it firmly. With a roar he threw the truck into gear and they jounced on up the road.

Hutch watched the road for any sign that other humans had penetrated this mountain fastness before them, but his only reward was a few deer droppings. In its time Fargo had been a thriving town, but that time had passed with the silver and now only the coons and the rats recalled its presence. Hutch checked the 1934 map he had swiped from the public library in Santa Fe, and nodded. They were definitely on the right road.

Twenty minutes later, the town loomed up before them. Gray-silvery wood buildings clung haphazardly to the side of the mountain and rambled sadly down to the edge of a stream that bubbled loudly through the silence. To the right and slightly higher on the mountain than the town was the black slash of the mine opening. Hutch shut off the engine, and he and Sherry regarded the bleak sight.

"Where do you think the dump would have been?"

"Downstream would be my guess," replied Hutch. "They wouldn't have wanted to haul their garbage up the side of the mountain."

Sherry shoved open the door of the cab and jumped to the ground. Hutch followed, but paused to pull down the shotgun that hung over the seat. A sudden wind whipped down from the peaks, sending a loose shutter banging hysterically against the side of a house. Sherry gave a cry and started, then looked embarrassed.

"Sorry."

"That's okay. I'm jumpy as a cat too."

They continued to hike downstream. Hutch

spotted a faint trail branching off from the main road. He nudged Sherry. With a nod she followed him down the hidden way. A half-mile down the trail they found the dump. The wind and weather of fifty years had done its work well, for the refuse was eroded and scattered.

"Well, there's nothing here that would make a self-respecting fly happy." Sherry sighed.

"Yeah, no 'rotting filth,' no 'foul sewage'" added Hutch, quoting Fonseca's description of the environment preferred by flies.

Sherry suddenly began to laugh at the incongruity of it all. Hutch's tanned face split into an answering smile, and setting the safety, he propped the shotgun against a tree and pulled her into his arms. The kiss was long, deep, and hungry, for with the worry and tension they hadn't made love for several days.

"You ever done it in a sleeping bag?" Hutch whispered against her ear.

"Once, and it was a disaster."

"You willin' to try it again?"

She glanced up at him, her eyes dancing with mischief and lust. "For certain results I'll try something even two or three times."

"Mighty glad to hear it. Shall we look for a place to camp, then?"

"Yes, but..." She hesitated and a shadow seemed to fall across her face. "Not near here. I don't want to be near any of these towns - just in case."

"Right," he answered shortly. Gripping the rifle in one hand, he hugged her tightly to his side as they hurried through the trees and back to the dubious safety of the truck.

They drove past nightfall, but at last Hutch located a small clearing near the stream that had been their companion in Fargo. Neither, was very hungry, but Sherry opened a can of corned beef and they forced down bites of sandwich with sips of the cold mountain water.

"We need rain," said Sherry, looking at the rocks of the stream bed that lay exposed above the waterline.

"We got extra hay because it held off this year." offered Hutch.

"Yeah, but what's going to be around to eat it next year?" Bitterness and despair edged her voice.

Hutch leaned over and pulled her down onto his open sleeping bag. "Hey, none of that now. First of all, we're gonna whip them suckers, but tonight we're not going to talk or think about anything but us. Deal?"

"Deal," she said, softly reaching up to trace his jawline with one finger.

Her hand slid to his belt and began to languidly tug at the buckle. His grin was wolfish in the moonlight as he slowly unbuttoned her blouse and pushed it off her shoulders. The buckle sagged and the zipper rasped swiftly downward. Her hands moved deftly within his pants, and he gave a gasp, then crushed his mouth onto hers. They wriggled frantically out of their Levi's and underwear.

"Ouch!"

"What?" Sherry giggled.

"Rolled off the bag. Those damn pine needles are *sharp.*"

"Poor baby." She laughed at his aggrieved tone, then with a growl pulled him down onto her.

His hands began a slow stroking progress across her damp body, but she shook her head in a sharp gesture of negation and seized his member in both hands, forcing it into her.

"Love me!" she ordered. "Love me hard and *now.*"

He gripped her tight against him and thrust deep into her. She moaned with pleasure and her lips played across his shoulders as he hammered ever deeper into her. Suddenly he became aware that another wetness had joined the touch of her mouth on his skin. Tears glistened on her face.

He almost spoke, but realized that no words could comfort her. Only the continuation of their life dance could ease her, so he buried his head in her soft bosom and loved her.

He woke to the pungent smell of pine smoke and frying bacon. Sore muscles twinged protestingly, and Hutch thought longingly of Sherry's wide double bed or even his bunk in the small adobe bunkhouse where he had lived for so many years.

"Glad you could join the living, lazy bones. It's almost seven o'clock," called Sherry from the side of the stream where she was washing her face in the cold water.

"You let that bacon burn, woman, and you'll be sorry that I've joined you," Hutch threatened as he stood and stretched.

"Don't worry." She crossed to the fire and took out eggs from the cooler. "These are our last eggs."

"Think we ought to head back to civilization and restock?" asked Hutch hopefully as he splashed in the stream.

She shook her head, the fine golden strands of her hair covering her face. "No. We've got enough canned goods to last for another couple of days."

"We've been out here for four days already."

"I know, but I begrudge the time to go back and start out again. I just feel that time is of the essence."

"Okay, you're the boss."

"And don't you forget it," she said, tossing her hair back. Then, more seriously, she added, "Maybe we'll find it today."

But they didn't. Nor did they in the following two days. Hutch dropped the brittle old map, watching expressionlessly as it fluttered softly onto the seat of the truck.

"That's it."

Sherry stared at him, her blue eyes pleading with him not to give up, not to destroy her hope. He hardened his heart against her and resolutely shook his head.

"We've hit every town on the map. There's no place else to try."

"But, Hutch, they have to be here."

"But they're not!" he shouted, jerking around on the seat. Nerves frayed from tension and too little sleep gave way, and he found himself shaking her in his frustration.

Her eyes started to fill with tears, then her jaw tightened and her hand flashed up, catching him hard across the face. He drew back, startled, and ruefully rubbed at his stinging cheek.

"Trust you not to respond like any other female in creation." And his slow smile lit his face.

The anger and tension ebbed from her body and she smiled in response. "I knew I had to get your attention," she said with a little shrug.

"Did you have to get it quite so - er - forcefully?"

She leaned forward and brushed the tan cheek with her lips. "Is that better?"

"Much."

"Now, let's think. Are we really dead in the water, or could there be a town that didn't make it onto that map?"

Hutch leaned back and closed his eyes, allowing his mind to range over thirty years of wanderings over New Mexico and Colorado. Scenes flashed before him. That terrible April when he was eight and the blizzard had roared down out of the Rockies. He remembered how he and his father had ridden through the drifts digging out dead and dying calves. He remembered deer hunting and the beautiful twelve-point buck who had come up in his sights, but he had let him go because he was too proud and perfect to kill. That memory triggered another, and he jerked upright and stared at Sherry.

"What?" she cried, worried by his expression. "Quick! Was there a Trinidad on any of these maps?"

"I... I don't know." She began to frantically shuffle through the tattered sheets. "Why?"

"There is another town up here. I found it once when I was hunting for a renegade mountain lion. We've seen a lot of ghost towns, I know, but none of them seem to have the setting of this one."

Sherry's eyes devoured the yellowed maps, checking each red circle, which marked another town discovered and discarded. "No Trinidad," she said at last.

"Then we're not out of the game yet. That town was isolated, but it was reasonably close to several ranching communities. It's possible that they still might be using the Trinidad dump. We can hope anyway."

"Oh, Hutch, you're a genius," Sherry cried, hugging him to her. "I just pray God that this is the place."

"And I just pray God that we get out of there alive if it is," Hutch mumbled against her hair.

"What?"

"Nothing."

Chapter Twelve

"Looks like we walk from here," said Hutch as they stared morosely out of the dirty windshield at the tangle of weeds and stones that the road had vanished into.

"Okay." Sherry hopped down from the truck and sniffed the air. "Smells like there might be a change in the weather coming."

"Uh," Hutch grunted noncommittally. He wasn't one for hunches or intuition, but there was something about the area that had the hair on the back of his neck crawling. Somehow the two shells that he kept in the chamber of the shotgun no longer seemed enough. Reaching beneath the seat of the truck, he pulled out a box of shells and began feeding them into the shell carrier on the butt of the rifle. Even the five extra shells now riding on the butt didn't seem sufficient, so he dug out a handful and thrust them into his pocket for good measure.

"Ready?"

"Yep, now I am," he answered, slamming the door shut. The sound echoed ominously in the high peaks that surrounded them.

"Any idea which way we go?" Sherry asked.

"Straight on for right now. That's the way the road seemed to be pointing. Be sure to listen for water, though. These folks always built along a water supply. If we can find a stream or spring, we can find the town."

Sherry nodded her understanding, and they set out. The clearing gave way to forest. Tall pines and scrub oak battled for room, and the rotting pine needles that carpeted the ground muffled their footfalls.

Suddenly Sherry stopped and gestured for silence. She listened intently for several minutes, then said, "I think I can hear water off to our left."

"Worth a try. We could spend a lifetime wandering around in here."

After a few more minutes of walking, even Hutch could hear the splash and babble of water as it tumbled over stones. The trees straggled to an end and they found themselves in a small mountain meadow dominated by a round-topped weathered hillock at the far end. The stream emerged from the forest and cut diagonally across the grassy field. And clustered about it were a number of crumbling adobe houses.

"I gather this wasn't a mining community," Sherry said.

"No, seems to have been a Spanish village, but the people just up and left or vanished one day."

Sherry bent and dug a china cup out of the moist earth. "Perfectly intact. How strange that they would leave it behind." She shaded her eyes with one hand and peered toward the hill. "What's that on top of the hill?"

Hutch lifted the pair of binoculars he had slung over his neck. "Big wooden cross. 'Bout fallen down, though."

"Well, let's move on."

Ten minutes later they had crossed the meadow, rounded the base of the hill, and virtually stumbled over the most intact building in the abandoned village. The church rose two stories over their heads. Paneless windows gaped sadly out over the peaceful meadow, and an angry meadowlark dive-bombed the couple from her nest, set high in one of the windows. At one time the church had possessed two towers set on each corner of the front of the building, but they had fallen into heaps of mud at the foot of the church and all that remained were skeletal board frames to which the adobe had been applied.

One massive carved wooden front door had been partially torn from its hinges, and Sherry slipped through the opening into the shadowed nave. Hutch jumped forward and tried to catch her arm before she could enter. Cursing at his near miss, he hesitated on the threshold. He hadn't liked this area from the minute he'd climbed out of the truck, and the discovery of the abandoned church was doing nothing to improve his feeling of unease.

"Hutch, come here. This is amazing."

He shifted his rifle from arm to arm and hesitated. "Hutch!"

"Okay," he shouted, and plunged in. Lifting his eyes toward the altar, he stared into the agonized eyes of a Christ hung over the rotting altar.

"Jesus," he whispered, and felt immediately foolish. "Exactly," Sherry answered, "but look at this." She was staring up at the choir loft over the back of the church, shading her eyes against the sunlight that streamed in through a window and reflected brilliantly off a series of pipes. "That is an absolutely incredible pipe organ, and here it is lost and forgotten in the mountains of New Mexico."

"Speaking of lost and forgotten, I don't want to join this organ in becoming a permanent resident up here," muttered Hutch. "Don't you think we ought to get on with the job so we can get back to civilization? Especially since we're almost out of food."

"Couldn't we just see if it works? Please, Hutch?"

"Sherry!" he howled, but as always, her eyes pleaded and he gave in. "Oh, okay. What do we have to do?"

"The keyboard is up by the altar, and there ought

to be a set of bellows either hand or foot operated."

"And I get to operate the bellows, right?"

"Right." She giggled at his long-suffering tone.

The system made alarming noises as air was once more run into it, but when Sherry pressed down a dirt-encrusted key, miraculously a full resonant note echoed through the vault of the church. It died with a whimper, however, and Sherry snatched her hand back guiltily.

"Well, I guess it's amazing that it made any sound at all."

"Yeah. Now let's get out of here, okay?"

Protected by the heavy adobe walls of the church, they had been unaware of the change in the weather during their explorations. Boiling black clouds tumbled over the mountain peaks pushed by a screaming, hissing wind that swept through the valley. The wind, whipping the words from their mouths, carried on it the scent of carnage.

"Oh, God!" Sherry gagged and covered her mouth with one hand.

"I think we found it," Hutch shouted as he stared north from whence came the terrible scent.

The man shifted the rifle from the crook of his arm into a combat grip. Slowly the couple moved toward a high ridge, and the source of the odor. Near the top of the rocky ridge Hutch threw himself onto his belly and motioned Sherry to do the same. Then slowly, painfully, on elbows and knees he wriggled to the top. Sherry arrived only seconds later, and together they gazed into the great pit.

It was obvious from the great mounds of rotting debris that the dump had been in constant use by the ranchers and farmers of the area. It was just as obvious from the cars and trucks parked on the north end of the pit that several people had come to dump and had never escaped. For, indeed, they had found the nest.

Hutch and Sherry stared down into a black sea

that rolled and seethed in unholy life. Thousands of shiny bodies crawled over one another, or rose in sudden clouds of flight, only to drop once more to feed and burrow in the filth that was their natural habitat. The buzzing could be heard even over the howl of the wind, and Sherry buried her face in the crook of her arm and tried to cover her ears.

Hutch placed his lips to her ear. "It doesn't look like there've been any mutations, does it?"

Sherry struggled to speak, then gave up and simply nodded.

"Now that we've found them, let's get the hell out of here and get back to Fonseca. Since we've discovered that the first spraying didn't do any harm, maybe now he can find a spray that will kill the fuckers." Sherry's eyes were riveted on the pitiful cluster of trucks at the edge of the dump. "Do you suppose that any of those people could be..."

"Alive? Not a prayer, and if we're not gonna join them, we'd better not push our luck by staying up here. Fonseca said they could sense fresh blood. Probably only the storm's kept them off us this long."

Hutch pushed up onto his elbows, ready to make the long crawl back down the ridge. Suddenly the clouds overhead were ripped with a bolt of forked lightning. The lurid yellow light shot across the seething green and black bodies, making them shine with a hellish brilliance.

Sherry half-rose to her knees and gave a cry of terror as she pointed at a mound of garbage that had begun to shiver and quake as something boiled out from beneath. Bits of filth rolled down the sides of the mound like the eruption of some obscene volcano. Then from the ruins rose a gigantic fly. Some two to three feet in length, the creature crawled laboriously up from the pit directly toward the stunned couple. The eyes, like giant glittering coins, reflected their images back at them a thousand times over.

"Run!" bellowed Hutch, and he dived for the bottom of the ridge. Sherry whirled and shot after him. She skittered down the incline, feeling the loose rock and shale slithering from beneath her booted feet. Behind her she could hear the piercing buzz of the horde as it rose into action, and below it the ominous deep thrum of the monster fly.

She hit the grassy plain, and the sudden balance shift was too much for her. She went down in a panicky cartwheel of arms and legs. Sherry lay gasping, struggling to pull air into her starved lungs. The fall had knocked the wind from her and left her breathless.

At last she managed to roll onto her back and lever herself onto her elbows.

A nightmare was descending. Great bent and hairy legs with filth clinging to the fibrous hairs shivered above her, and above that worked a great sucking proboscis. Nausea and terror rose in her throat as Sherry pictured that instrument of death driving deep into her vulnerable body.

"Hutch!" she screamed, but she feared her cry had been lost in the crash of thunder.

The terrifying cacophony directly above him caused Hutch to start and half-turn back. It was then he realized that Sherry was not behind him. He spun around, already crouched for action, and stared in horror at the creature descending on his woman.

He threw the rifle to his shoulder, snapping off two shots in the fastest firing of his life. Before the report had died, he had broken the barrel and was flinging two more cartridges into the breach. Snapping it shut, he fired again. And he didn't miss.

Sherry shrieked in terror and disgust as the right eye of the fly disintegrated into a mass of goo. She heard two more shots, and the left eye vanished and a great hole was torn in the underbelly of the creature. A foul, greenish fluid spurted from the wound, covering her body with its fetid stickiness.

Hutch raced back to her, and seizing her under the armpits, he heaved her onto her feet. The heavens opened and a gray torrent battered at their heads and shoulders. Hand in hand, almost blinded by the fury of the rain, they fled back past the church and the quiet houses and raced for the trees.

The drumming of the rain and the almost constant thunderclaps made it impossible to discern if they were pursued. Hutch decided that it was best to assume pursuit, and clinging to Sherry, he ran like hell.

They realized they had reached the forest when trees began to whip their faces. Beneath the pines the darkness was almost total, and Hutch cursed himself for leaving the flashlight.

"Which way is the truck?" Sherry gasped, trembling from cold. As with all mountain cloudbursts, the temperature had plummeted with the onslaught of rain.

"I'm... I'm not sure," Hutch panted, "but instinct tells me that way." He thrust with his chin to their right, and they plowed off in that direction.

The flight was a nightmare of burning lungs and twisted ankles as they raced blindly through the forest. Then the trees began to thin, and before them they saw the pickup, ghostly in the gloom.

"Oh, thank God!" Sherry sobbed, then gave a sudden cry as a sharp stinging attacked the back of her neck.

"They're almost on us!" shouted Hutch. "Run! God, run!"

The rain had begun to lessen, and behind them they could now hear the hideous buzzing of the flies. The truck seemed to waver in a field of red as Hutch's overworked lungs struggled to carry him the last few feet to the vehicle. Sherry was a flopping weight dragging at his left hand, and the rifle seemed to have turned to stone.

He couldn't halt his forward momentum and slammed into the door. Dropping Sherry's hand, he fumbled for the handle and jerked open the truck door.. Pulling her past him, he seized her by the back of her pants and flung her headlong into the cab. Almost sobbing with exhaustion, he climbed in after her and slammed shut the door.

The flies battered themselves to death on the unyielding glass. Hutch rested for only a moment, then switched on the ignition and, flinging the truck into gear, roared out of the mountain clearing.

It was a long way to the highway that would take them back to Los Alamos with the news of the nest, and with the knowledge that they had all feared. There had been a mutation, and now time was running out.

Chapter Thirteen

Los Alamos looked normal. The buildings stood glittering in the early-morning sunlight. The water in the pond in the central park ruffled lightly, pushed by a gentle breeze, but there were no people. The eerie silence was beginning to affect Hutch, and clutching the steering wheel, he peered through the filthy windshield at the empty street.

"Hutch, look."

He followed the direction of Sherry's finger and stared in dismay at six small bloody masses on the sidewalk near the park.

"What are they?"

"They look like ducks," she said quietly, and tears filled her eyes as she remembered the last time they had driven this road and she had watched the fat waddling ducks taking bread from children's hands. "The flies must have attacked. Oh, God! Then they're dead, that means everyone is dead!" Hysteria sent her voice spiraling up, and Hutch leaned over and swiftly slapped her.

"Now stop that!" he yelled into her startled face, not bothering to watch the road. "We ain't seen any human bodies yet, and surely if the flies got 'em, they'd be all over the place."

"That's true," Sherry whispered.

"Let's just get to Fonseca's and find out what the score is."

The parking lot at Fonseca's building was jammed with cars. Double parking, they locked the truck and hurried into the building. The foyer was empty, the dragon absent from her desk. Relieved but puzzled, they walked quickly through the halls to Fonseca's lab.

Hutch's knock brought no response. The couple exchanged glances, then Sherry tried the handle. It turned easily and they entered the room. Fonseca had his back to them and he was peering into an enormous microscope.

"'Robert?" Sherry said softly.

He whirled about on the lab stool and stared at them with an almost maniacal expression out of reddened eyes. "I thought you were dead," he croaked hoarsely.

"Robert, what's happened here?" cried Sherry, hurrying to his side.

He clutched her hand and pressed it against his cheek momentarily. The contact seemed to calm him, for when he lifted his head once more, he seemed like the old Fonseca.

"The flies attacked, but they misjudged their target." He smiled grimly, an ugly expression on his gaunt face. "We're used to being ready for split-second emergencies up here, and fortunately we had enough warning to get everyone to shelters. I think our only casualties were some dogs and cats."

"And the ducks," Sherry said inanely from where she squatted by his chair absently stroking his hand. "What? Oh, yes, in the park."

"Haven't you had any rest since the attack?"

"No. It makes it harder somehow, knowing that it's your responsibility. And I'm no closer to an answer."

"And you're not going to find an answer if you don't get some rest. There wasn't a fly in sight out there, so you're going home." Sherry rose and tugged the older man to his feet.

"Oh, the attack's been over for several days. It's just that everyone is staying close to home or lab."

"Makes sense," Hutch said, taking the scientist by the other arm, and together he and Sherry propelled Fonseca toward the door.

"Did you find anything?" he asked suddenly, his head turning from one to the other.

"Yep."

"Nope."

Hutch and Sherry's words tangled in each other, and they halted, glaring at each other.

"Well tell you after you've had some food and rest," Sherry said firmly.

They reached the parking lot at last and located Fonseca's Cadillac.

"Where do you live?" asked Sherry.

"Twenty-three hundred Aspen Lane, but I can drive," he protested feebly as Hutch dug the keys from his coat pocket.

"Nonsense, just direct us," Sherry snapped as she shoved him into the front seat.

Fonseca's house was on the extreme north end of the town, tucked away in the mountains that surrounded Los Alamos. An imposing redwood structure, it looked as if the house had been built to accommodate the granite boulders and tall pines that encompassed the building.

They left the car at the foot of hewn sandstone stairs that led to the arching fifteen-foot door. Inside, high skylights sent streams of light flooding down over stark modernistic furnishings.

Hutch looked at the two exhausted people facing him and said, "Can I suggest that we all hit the hay? Sherry and I have driven all night, and you look like you haven't rested for twice that long, Doc. We can always rustle up something to eat later."

"A good idea. I'll show you to a room."

They followed Fonseca up a curving staircase to the second story. Their room was on the left, near the head of the stairs. The room was simply furnished with a bookcase bed against one natural-wood wall, and facing a wide sliding glass door that opened out onto a veranda. Hutch settled onto the bed and gave a yelp of surprise as it rocked beneath him.

"Water bed," explained Fonseca.

"Oh," Hutch said, expressions of lust and embarrassment warring for control.

Fonseca left, and Hutch and Sherry quickly stripped and stepped into the large shower. The beat of the hot water and the gentle massage of Hutch's hands squeezed the tension out of the woman. With a smile she took the bar of soap from him and washed his firm hard body with long languid sweeps.

Once in bed, they soon became accustomed to the roll and gurgle of the mattress, and Hutch slipped a bare arm about her waist.

"Sure is going to be somethin' makin' it in a water bed," mumbled Hutch. "I feel like I'm in some dirty movie..." His voice sank slowly away and blended into indistinguishable snores.

Sherry listened for several minutes, then slipped into sleep.

She awoke suddenly out of nightmare and found herself with neither the comfort of Hutch's arm nor the covers, for he had stolen them all and wrapped them about himself, cocoon-fashion. From the twilight outside she reckoned it to be around eight o'clock. She felt a stab of guilt at the time they had spent sleeping when time was so critical, but she justified it with the argument that soon they would have to face the governor again and they would need all their strength.

Slipping from the bed, she started to pad toward the door, but was caught by a glimmer of white in the darkness. She paused and lifted the gossamer material.

It was a delicate robe, and she wondered how many women Fonseca must have to this house to keep a wardrobe on hand for them. She blushed at the thought as she drew on the robe and moved to the veranda.

She allowed the door to slide quietly shut behind her, and she moved to the veranda railing. The moon was just rising over the peaks in front of her, and its silver light threw weird shadows into the canyon that yawned at her feet. She drew back slightly when she realized that the deck was built over the nothingness, of a mountain gorge, and then sensed someone's presence.

Fonseca was a shadow in the darkness. He wore a knee-length brown linen robe, his hands thrust deep into the pockets. A glowing cigarette dangled between his lips. There was enough light to illuminate his face, and Sherry saw a brooding sadness there as he gazed at her. Suddenly she became aware of the sheerness of the robe, and she drew it tighter about her body.

"I'm sorry, I shouldn't have sneaked up on you like that," he said, seeming to read her unease.

"Thank you for the robe."

He shrugged, and taking the cigarette from his mouth, he exhaled smoke in a long gray stream. "The fruits of a playboy existence," he said, and there was a wealth of bitterness in the sentence.

"Why are you alone?" asked Sherry, moving back to the railing. "Why haven't you ever married?"

"Personal choice, and one which I'm beginning to regret."

She whirled, her back against the rail. Fonseca was very close, and she could smell a combination of aftershave and bourbon. Strangely it was as pleasant in its way as the odor of tobacco and sweat that she had come to associate with Hutch, and she didn't try to move away.

"I'm a scientist, and science is my god, my mistress. I came here, built this house, peopled it with

my books, and thought I would be happy. And I was...
for a while."

"So what happened?"

"I met a woman who seemed to be life incarnate...
and I realized how sterile my existence was without
you."

The hot blood rushed into her face, and she found
herself stammering. "I... I didn't-"

He cut her off with a quick shake of his head. "I
don't mean to upset you or make you uncomfortable. I
know what you share with Hutch, but I had to tell you
what you've done to me." He stepped away from her,
leaning heavily on the rail as he gazed into the canyon's
black depths. She watched the tiny shower of orange
sparks fall away into darkness as he tossed the cigarette
over the edge.

Suddenly he turned back to face her. "May I kiss
you?"'

Mutely she nodded. He stepped forward and
pulled her into his arms. If was a powerful kiss, more
expert than Hutch's, and it affected her-far more than she
liked.

"Thank you. I won't ask that of you again unless
we all come through this alive. Then..." He paused and
shrugged. "Well, then we'll see."

"Robert, we found the nest."

"I know. I suppose I sensed it. That's probably
what brought all this on."

"There've been mutations." The words hung
baldly between them and his eyes widened in fear.

"What?"

She nodded. "I don't know how many of them
there are, but Hutch killed a fly that was a good two or
three feet in length."

"The problem isn't how many there are now. The
problem is how many there'll be once they begin to lay.
Get Hutch up. We've got to get to the governor tonight."

Even though it was nearly ten o'clock the Round House was lit up as though the legislature were in session.

"Maybe the governor's actually working on the problem," growled Hutch from the passenger side of Fonseca's El Dorado.

"Lot of good it will do them. They never contacted *me*" Robert answered bitterly.

He parked the car, and they hurried to the front door of the building. They were met by an expressionless guard who jerked the glass door away from Sherry as she tried to open it.

"Nobody's allowed in at this hour. Make an appointment or come back tomorrow."

"But we have to see the governor," argued Sherry. "This is Dr. Robert Fonseca, and-"

"Oh, yeah. I have orders about you guys - and they don't include letting you in." He grinned sarcastically and pulled the door shut, slamming the lock home.

Sherry slumped down on the top step of the capitol and looked desperately up at the two men. "What do we do now?"

"Camp," Fonseca said laconically. "Somebody with some authority is bound to come out sooner or later."

"Want me to go out for pizza?" quipped Hutch, and laughing, they settled down on the stairs.

The wait was shorter than they expected. Within fifteen minutes the glass doors were shoved violently open by a spare, brown-haired man who bit down on his thin cigar as if trying to kill it. He seemed somewhat taken aback by the sight of three people blocking the steps of the capitol, and for several seconds the foursome just stared at one another. Hutch finally identified the man from news stories.

"Uh... uh, Chief Wilson, right?" he stammered,

lurching to his feet.

"Yes?" One eyebrow lifted questioningly and the tone was tinged with impatience.

"Uh... I'm Hutch Engels, and, uh..." He cast a desperate glance at his companions.

Fonseca moved smoothly into the breach. "Chief Wilson, I'm Dr. Robert Fonseca from Los Alamos laboratories. I'm certain we present a rather odd image perched on the doorstep like a pack of gypsies, but I assure you we have good reason." He paused, looking to Sherry for inspiration.

"We need to see the governor," she prompted.

"Ah, yes. Well, the fact of the matter is that we need to speak with the governor."

"So go in and talk to him," broke in Wilson.

"The... er... difficulty is that the governor has left orders that we not be admitted, but it is imperative that we see him."

"Why?" The tone was harsh and challenging.

Fonseca stepped back and evaluated his opponent. There was steel in the gray eyes, but the scientist thought he read fairness there as well. He decided to level with the police officer.

"We know about the fly crisis." He paused, summoning courage. "In fact, I'm the man who is responsible for their creation. My friends have discovered information vital to the destruction of these creatures, but we must reach the governor,"

Wilson slowly removed the cigar and spat over the edge of the steps. He seemed to study the scientist in the same calculating way that Fonseca had used earlier, then abruptly he nodded.

"I can get you in, but it probably won't do you a hell of a lot of good."

"Why not?" interrupted Sherry.

"That man" - Wilson's arm thrust out sword-like at the building behind him-"is a dithering idiot. I've just left a five-hour meeting where nothing was decided and nothing was accomplished. One minute we're going to call in the feds, then in the next breath everyone is worrying about the elections, so the call isn't made. If you can say something that will get that jackass to *move*, then I'll get you in."

"Believe me, the information we have would get action out of a corpse, Chief Wilson," said Fonseca fervently. "Okay, let's go. What the hell, it's only my job." Whirling, he pushed open the doors and led them into the capitol. The guard they had encountered earlier rushed forward, but he retreated swiftly at the expression on Wilson's face. Soon they stood before the governor's office door.

"Is he alone?" Hutch asked.

"No, several of his aides are with him, which might be to your advantage if you can convince Lewis Dobson. I'm beginning to think he may be the real power in the government right now."

The two men nodded. Sherry simply stared silently and intently at the door. Wilson stepped forward and shoved open the door.

"Frank! Glad you reconsidered and decided to stick with us," boomed out a clipped, military-sounding voice.

Wilson didn't answer, just stepped aside, allowing the three people behind him to enter the room.

Philip Archuleta looked up from his desk and gave a moan of despair. "Oh, no, it's them again." His face was deathly white and his hands shook violently as he struggled to light a cigarette. An aide leaped to his side, flicking on a lighter.

"Who are these people?" demanded an erect gray-haired man. Sherry recognized the voice as the man who had first greeted the police chief.

She could feel Hutch and Robert staring at her, but she imperceptibly shook her head and stepped back.

This wasn't the time for a woman, no matter how strongly motivated, to speak out. It would take someone with credibility and authority to convince the four hard-faced men in the office that action had to be taken, and immediately. She turned to Fonseca and touched him on the shoulder. It was a pleading little gesture. He grasped her fingers briefly and gave them a quick reassuring squeeze.

"Gentlemen, I am Dr. Robert Fonseca. As the governor already knows"-he flicked an accusing glance at the gaunt figure behind the desk-"I am the man who created the flies that are now menacing the state." There was an eruption of words from the three aides, but Dobson's parade-ground manner won out once more.

"Why wasn't I informed of this?" he virtually screamed at the cowering Archuleta.

"I just... didn't think."

"Obviously!" The word lashed across the room and the governor flinched.

"Please," cried Fonseca, holding up a hand to forestall any further outbursts. "This is a waste of time and we don't have any to waste. These people" - he indicated Sherry and Hutch - "have been working with me. Thanks to their heroic efforts, they have located the flies' nest."

"But that's wonderful news," burbled Dobson. "With this information we can pinpoint the spraying and deal with the beasts."

"Not so fast, sir," rasped Fonseca. "I warned the governor days ago against this ill-advised spraying. I wasn't heeded, and now we're about to reap the fruits of that decision."

"What are you blathering about? Would you get to the point?" ordered Dobson, impatient with Fonseca's professorial manner.

The scientist reddened under the insult, then plunged ahead. "Sherry and Hutch have observed not only the flies' nest, but a mutation caused by the spraying, just as I predicted."

"What was the mutation?" queried Bruce Pearson, his blue eyes staring with terror.

"Sherry was attacked by a fly over two feet in length," Fonseca said grimly. "Fortunately Hutch was able to destroy the creature before it killed her."

"Were any other of these mutations observed?" asked Dobson dryly.

"No," said Sherry suddenly, "but that doesn't mean that there aren't more of them out there."

"Besides," broke in Fonseca, "the issue isn't how many of the mutations are out there now. The issue is that we are approaching the laying season." He paused, allowing his listeners to digest that bit of information. "You mean these creatures are about to-"

"Reproduce? Exactly, and since each female fly can lay up to a thousand eggs a year, we are soon going to be ass-deep in giant carnivorous flies."

Dobson sank back into his chair, his face as white as the governor's. "Phil," he said softly, "I think the decision has been taken from us. This is more than we can handle. We've got to call Washington."

The room was silent as Archuleta gazed at each person in the room, begging, pleading, searching for a reprieve. There was none.

"My election," he sighed, almost too low to be heard. "María, I would have won it for you," he whispered, and the words died like a faint cry of a dying animal.

Slowly he reached for the phone on the desk and pulled it to him.

Chapter Fourteen

The heavy *whump, whump, whump* of helicopter propellers filled the early morning. In the west the sun was just rising, and the glow set up a sort of reflexive effect across the entire sky. Hutch shaded his eyes and peered about, searching for the aircraft. At last he spotted them and pointed for the benefit of his companions.

The trio had been awakened at their hotel by a four-o'clock phone call from the governor's office telling them that the "party from Washington" was arriving shortly, and to order Sherry, Hutch, and Fonseca to the capitol as soon as possible.

They had stumbled into their clothes, but rather than going directly to the governor's office, they had decided to wait and watch the arrival. Apparently there had been a leak, for the lawn was filled with milling journalists and camera crews all armed with mini cams or Live Eyes or other portable camera equipment.

"I thought they would come by car," said Sherry as she watched the rapidly approaching helicopters.

"I think we're playing in the big leagues," responded Fonseca.

The craft were coming in out of the south, and the sound of the propellers rose to a screaming whine as they began to settle onto the lawn of the capitol.

Hutch and Fonseca both whistled in surprise when they identified the helicopters, for both were giant

Hueys, capable of carrying a squad. And indeed they seemed to be.

As the propellers began to slow, the doors on the first craft opened and twelve men in dark suits boiled out. Sherry was startled not only by their combat attitude, but also by the deadly UZI submachine guns they all carried.

"We're in the big time," Fonseca said again as he too looked at the guns.

There were fewer people in the second craft. Only three men with briefcases, and surrounded by four hard-eyed bodyguards, they climbed out and hurried toward the doors of the capitol.

"Jesus!" hissed Fonseca suddenly. "That's Harold Fallon, chief security adviser to the President."

"Is that good?" asked Hutch.

"Well, it can't hurt. They say that guy has more power than almost anyone else in the Executive."

"Oh," replied Hutch, feeling not very much more informed than before he'd asked, and decidedly out of place and ill-at-ease in his old Levi's and boots.

Off to Sherry's left a newsman began murmuring into his microphone. Suddenly the device was ripped from his hands by one of the black-suited individuals and ground into splinters beneath a heel.

"Hey!" shouted the newsman before he was spun roughly about and shoved toward the news vans.

Pandemonium was breaking out all across the lawn as news people were hustled toward their cars. Over the shouts was the sound of shattering equipment as expensive cameras were thrown to the ground or beaten firmly to pieces with the butts of guns. In contrast to the screaming, gesticulating journalists, the federal escort men seemed cool, almost bored, with the proceedings.

Sherry, Hutch, and Fonseca stood on the outskirts of the melee, watching the battle in fascinated horror.

Their immunity ended suddenly and brutally when one of the gun-toting feds grabbed Sherry by the upper arm and shoved her violently toward the street. With a cry she sprawled face down on the grass. Hutch gave a snarl and launched himself at the agent. He took him hard in the back of the knees, and they both went down in a tangle of arms and legs.

Hutch swung with his right fist, a blow that would have broken the man's jaw, had it connected, but the agent blocked the blow and gripped the rancher by the throat. Hutch flung himself over in an attempt to break the strangling hold, and they went rolling across the grass. A second fed, seeing his comrade's difficulties, rushed across the lawn and smashed the barrel of his UZI across the side of Hutch's head. Blood blossomed along the line of the cut, matting the blond hair and dripping from his chin.

Fonseca, looking desperately from side to side, saw Bruce Pearson step from the capitol and stare aghast at the aftermath of the now-diminishing battle. Ducking his head, the scientist raced across the grass toward the steps. A dark-suited fed loomed up before him, but Fonseca hit him a glancing blow with one shoulder and the man went flying. He staggered up the steps and leaned on the door frame, gasping for breath. Mentally he cursed himself for being so out-of-condition.

Fonseca turned to Pearson, and the young man began to retreat nervously for the door. The older man's hand shot out and gripped the aide by the wrist, dragging him face to face with the scientist.

"My friends," Fonseca croaked. "Tell them we're with you, for God's sake!"

"I... I..."

"Do it!" he roared, and shoved Pearson down the steps.

The governor's aide trotted across the lawn, fluttering his hands at the crowd that had gathered around Sherry and Hutch. Hutch was kneeling groggily on the ground, slowly shaking his head. Sherry, who had tried to go to his aid, was pinned against one of the agents with her arms pulled tightly behind her back.

"Please, please," murmured Pearson. "These people are associated with the governor's office."

The agent looked with disinterest from Sherry and Hutch to the sweating Pearson. "Then why were they out here watching Mr. Fallon and his party?"

"Are you terminally paranoid or what?" spat Sherry, twisting in the man's grip. "We had just arrived from our hotel and we hadn't had time to go in yet." Her voice was thick with disgust.

"Mr. Fallon is already inside and these people are needed for the briefing."

With a shrug the man stepped back, releasing Sherry. She rushed to Hutch and dropped down next to him, taking his face gently between her hands.

"Are you all right?"

"Unfortunately I think I'm gonna live," he quipped, and tried to smile. But the effort pulled the facial cut, and his expression faded into one of pain.

Supported by Sherry's shoulder, Hutch regained his feet, and they tottered toward the door. Fonseca watched them coming, a strange expression on his face. As they reached the steps, he came down and took Hutch's other arm. Together, he and Sherry supported him into the capitol, followed by the subdued Pearson.

Fonseca and Hutch vanished into the second-floor restroom to tend to Hutch's face while Pearson escorted Sherry to the governor's office.

The low murmur of male voices died away as she entered the room. The cast was the same as the day before, but now the three Washington officials had been added. Sherry's attention was drawn by the tall silver-haired man who had preempted Archuleta's desk. His startlingly blue eyes widened as he took in her appearance, and he carefully set his coffee cup back onto the saucer.

Sherry's lips twisted in a sardonic smile, and she wondered if he were taken with her beauty or the fact that her cheek was streaked with dirt and her blouse had a large grass stain across the front.

"And this is... ?" he asked Dobson, who was hovering about.

"Sherry Quinn, a rancher from up north."

"And why is she here?"

"Because my child was killed by the flies and because I've done more than anyone in this room to try to destroy them."

"That's a rather harsh indictment of the government's efforts, Mrs. Quinn."

"One that's deserved."

An uncomfortable silence fell over the room. Another of the Washington mob, as Sherry had mentally dubbed them, stepped to Fallon's side. His intense black eyes were locked on Sherry, and he impatiently brushed back a forelock of dark hair that fell wildly across his face as he bent to his boss's ear. He whispered for several minutes, his eyes never leaving Sherry. When he concluded, Fallon made a slight negative gesture and motioned him away. Just when Sherry was about to scream from the silent tension, the door opened and Hutch and Fonseca entered. Gratefully she moved to their sides and took up a defensive position between them.

"Hutch Engels," said Dobson, this time not waiting to be ordered, "and Dr. Robert Fonseca."

Fallon's eyes flicked over Hutch and dismissed him as unimportant. "Ah, Doctor, I'm very pleased to be - meeting you at last. Your fine work at Los Alamos has brought you no little attention with the National Security Agency."

"I'm sure. It isn't every day that a government

scientist creates a menace to national security," Fonseca responded dryly.

"But you misunderstand me, Doctor. The government holds you entirely blameless in this whole affair."

"It does?" Fonseca asked warily.

"Oh, yes. But now I think we should begin. I'm certain that Colonel Baker will be arriving shortly."

Sherry glanced up at Robert and noticed that some of the tension had eased out of his face, to be replaced with an expression of deep relief. She was ill-at-ease among these men of power, and she feared the outcome of this meeting. Fallon motioned Fonseca to a chair near the desk, and involuntarily Sherry's hand tightened on his arm. She knew that she and Hutch were the outsiders here, and she was afraid that her ally was slipping back into the world that had produced him. She felt a surge of dread as she wondered how they would continue without Robert.

Fonseca hesitated at the pressure on his arm, then he gently broke free and took the indicated chair. Hutch and Sherry retreated to the back of the office and leaned uncomfortably against the wall, since there were no chairs left.

Fallon snapped his fingers, and his third aide pulled down a gigantic area map of New Mexico. "First allow me to explain our position. The President is obviously extremely concerned over these attacks, and one of his major fears is that the danger will spread beyond the confines of northern New Mexico. "Fortunately the attacks still seem to be localized in this area." He swept a pointer, supplied by the dark-haired and hostile young man, across the upper half of the map. "Therefore we propose intensive spraying across this entire area."

"But spraying didn't work before," objected Sherry. "It only led to mutations."

Fallon's urbane smile never slipped as he surveyed the blond woman. "True, but your national guard wasn't using the compound our pilots will be using."

"Then why spray the entire area? Hutch and I have located the nest. You could do a pinpoint spraying and avoid spreading that stuff all over the state."

"I deeply appreciate the work you and your friend have done, Mrs. Quinn, but if by chance not all of our flies are in the nest, the spraying will have been to no avail. Under the circumstances we feel that our way is better."

"But-"

Sherry's disagreement was cut short by a sharp knock on the office door.

"Ah, that must be Colonel Baker," said Fallon, and he motioned for the door to be opened. Both aides raced each other for the honor, and beside her, Sherry heard Hutch give a snort of disgust.

The man who entered was of medium height with broad shoulders, but a developing paunch marred the fit of his army uniform. He saluted briskly, then grinned and gave Fallon a thumbs-up signal.

"It's done?"

"Yes, sir. The canisters are at Kirtland Air Force Base."

"Well done, Colonel."

"What sort of insecticide are you using?" asked Fonseca.

"Nothing you've ever heard of, Doctor," Fallon began smoothly, "It's just been-"

"Raben," broke in the colonel, obviously eager to describe his toy. "And it's not an insecticide. It's a nerve gas developed by our boys up at the Rocky Mountain Arsenal."

"But that's a biological-warfare unit," muttered Fonseca, beginning to climb out of his chair.

"Of course."

"That will be all, Colonel Baker!" Fallon's voice snapped out across the room.

"Yes, sir." Chastised and beginning to realize that he had made an error, Baker retreated into a corner.

Archuleta, who had sat like a zombie through most of the proceedings, suddenly raised his head from his breast. "Nerve gas," he repeated dully.

"My God," whispered Fonseca. "You're going to kill the people too."

Fallon stared from person to person, noting the mounting horror in Sherry's eyes, the dulled disbelief in the governor's, and the naked fury in Fonseca's. With a shrug he dropped his affable, social manner. The pointer beat out a rapid tattoo on the map.

"Yes, Doctor, I'm afraid that is essentially the case."

"But all those people! Surely you can warn them, give them time to evacuate?" Sherry burst out.

"Regretfully, Mrs. Quinn, no. Our greatest enemy is time. The population in the region has been sharply reduced by the fly attacks. It is also very scattered. To try to warn and evacuate the people would take more time than we've got."

"It's barbaric," mumbled Archuleta.

Dobson stepped to his side and laid a calming hand on his shoulder. "I know it seems hard, sir, but we have to think beyond New Mexico. The nation is at stake."

With a weak nod the governor subsided. Sherry shot Dobson a look of loathing and turned on Fallon.

"What kind of government would murder its own people?"

"A sensible one," responded Fallon urbanely. "Think of it as triage."

"But it's not triage," shouted Fonseca, advancing on the impassive Fallon. "We're not talking about the waste of medical aid on soldiers who would die anyway. We're talking about the slaughter of innocents!"

"Your slaughter, Doctor. Remember the government can be as quick to blame as to forgive. Are you sure you want to assume that burden?" There was steel in Fallon's voice, and he wielded the pointer like a rapier, holding off Fonseca's advance.

"Robert, don't let him blackmail you!" Sherry cried desperately.

Fonseca wavered and buried his face in his hands. "I don't know. I don't know," he muttered brokenly.

"Well, I do," said Sherry coldly. "I'll find a way to destroy these flies before you can act. I'll never agree to this plan! You're not going to smear this blood on my hands as well."

"As you wish, Mrs. Quinn. But remember you have very little time. At sunrise tomorrow our planes will take off from Kirtland. That gives you a little less than twenty-four hours." He smiled thinly and pulled the pointer through his hands.

Sherry stared at Fonseca. "Is no one going to help me?" She felt Hutch step up beside her and grip her hand tightly in his. Tears filled her eyes at even this sign of expected support. "All right. Then it's up to Hutch and me, just the way it always was."

They wove through the silent men to the door. "Remember," said Fallon as her hand touched the knob. "Less than twenty-four hours. If you're up there, you'll die with everyone else."

"They're my neighbors. I'd rather die with them than live with people like you."

The door clicked softly shut.

Chapter Fifteen

The small adobe house behind its weathering pole fence lay quiet in the morning sun. Sherry jumped from the rented car even before it stopped rolling, and ran across the gravel drive to the front door. She noticed that Kathy had replaced the plain glass window in the door with an exquisite piece of stained glass, and she decided to ask where the journalist had found it. It was just what she wanted for the side window at home. With an angry jerk of her head she pulled herself back to reality. The purchase of a piece of stained glass belonged to a sane and rational world that no longer existed. She grasped the heavy brass door knocker beneath the window and hammered desperately at the door.

Oh, God, let her be at home. Please don't let her be in Los Alamos screwing Charles, or off chasing some story. I need her.

She continued the silent litany even as she persisted in pounding ferociously at the unyielding wood. "No answer?" asked Hutch.

"No."

"She's got to be here. Her car is in the garage."

"Unless Charles picked her up."

"Oh, yeah." Hutch's face fell morosely as he considered that possibility.

"Who the hell is it?" came a grumpy voice from the other side of the door.

"Kathy, it's Sherry! Open the door!"

The door was flung open and Sherry stumbled into the warm plant-filled foyer.

"Sherry! My God, you look like death warmed over. What's wrong?" The journalist wrapped her arms about her friend and pulled her into the cluttered living room. "Here, sit down." She grabbed a pile of books and prepared to toss them into a corner when Sherry caught her by the wrists.

"There's no time for that," snapped Sherry, unconsciously echoing Fallon's words. "Something terrible is about to happen, so just listen and do what you can."

Kathy dropped the books back onto the couch and stared tensely at her friend. "Okay, I'm ready."

"The governor has called in the federal government, and they're going to begin spraying the north country with virulent nerve gas called-" She hesitated and turned to Hutch.

"Raben."

"That's right, Raben."

"Wait, wait, this is too fast. I've got to have a notebook." Kathy scurried to an overloaded roll-top desk set in the curve of a bay window and returned with a pen and pad. "Okay."

"Anyway, they believe that this stuff will kill the flies, but it is also going to kill every living thing in the area."

The journalist's round face whitened as the full import hit her. She staggered slightly, and Hutch hurriedly placed an arm around her shoulders.

"Who's in charge of this operation?"

"A man named Fallon."

"Oh, God."

"I know, we're apparently going up against God or at least the Holy Ghost, but, Kathy, we've got to do something," cried Sherry. "He's backed up by some army colonel named Baker."

"When is the spraying to begin?"

"Tomorrow at sunrise the planes are going to take off from Kirtland," said Hutch grimly.

"Tomorrow! Jesus, that doesn't give us any time at all!"

"Is there any way to stop it?" begged Sherry.

"Sure. I'll get in touch with UPI and AP. We'll break the story tonight in every major paper in the country. That should stop them."

"Oh, Kathy, thank you." Sherry tightly hugged the brown-haired woman, then broke loose, heading for the door.

"Hey! Why so fast?"

"Just in case this doesn't work, Hutch and I are going to try to think of some way to get at that nest."

"Nest?" Kathy Littlebird jumped on the word eagerly.

"Not now! We'll be in touch."

"Wait! Where can I reach you?"

"Try La Posada, room twenty-three."

The front door boomed shut behind the couple, and Kathy pressed one hand to her forehead. Tightening the belt on her robe, she pattered on bare feet to her typewriter and rolled a sheet into the carriage. She frowned with concentration as she typed out her shorthand notes in an understandable form. She wanted to have her facts absolutely straight before she phoned Washington and New York.

She had just pulled the paper from the machine when the front door burst open and six men in dark suits boiled into the room. Kathy gave a shriek of terror, but one look convinced her that this was no robbery.

Stalling for time, she pointed toward her bedroom, and in a quavering voice said, "My purse is on the dresser. I don't have much money, but you can have it. Just please don't hurt me." As she spoke, she was surreptitiously folding the single sheet with her left hand. She leaped up from her chair and, using the motion as a blind, thrust the paper into the large dictionary near the typewriter. Her eyes fell on the notebook lying open on the desk, but she comforted herself that no one would be able to read her own personal shorthand.

The swivel chair crashed to the brick floor as Littlebird tried to dart past the two men who were advancing on her. One of the men caught her by the arm, however, and spun her around, slamming her into the edge of the desk. She gave a groan of pain as the sharp wood bit into her hips.

Her two captors held her pinned against the desk while a third man, obviously the leader, sauntered over to them. His white-blond hair was cropped so short that it seemed almost invisible, and she shuddered as his cold gray eyes raked dispassionately across her. Under his scrutiny she realized that her low-cut gown had slipped to one side, revealing a bosom. Embarrassed, she reached for the material, only to have her arm jerked roughly behind her back. Her breast flopped free once more.

"Bastard!" she muttered. The blond man made no response, but Kathy thought she could detect a slight grin on the face of one of the goons who held her.

"Where are your notes?" asked the leader as he lit a cigarette.

"Notes? I don't know what you're talking about," she replied, smiling sweetly up at him.

His fist shot out easily and crashed into her jaw. The soft flesh of her inner cheek was driven into her teeth, and tears of pain and fear filled her eyes.

"Notes," he repeated.

"I have lots of notes," she babbled around a glob of blood that was filling her mouth.

He sighed and righted her chair. "Please, let's not play games, Ms. Littlebird," he said as he seated himself.

"This can get a lot rougher and I don't think you're ready for that."

"You can't get away with this," she said. "I've got rights."

"True, if you were being held by a formal law enforcement agency, but we're not so affiliated. Now give me your notes. We know that Mrs. Quinn and Mr. Engels were here; they must have told you about our plans, and being a good little journalist, you must have made some notes."

Kathy drew in a deep breath and gave a stubborn shake of her head.

"All right, then, I guess we'll just have to find them." He gestured to the three remaining men, who began to ransack the house. Kathy stared in horror as the cushions of her couch were seized and ripped open along with the frame of the couch. Lamps were shattered and books were flung from the bookcases as the mindless search continued.

"This is crazy!" she suddenly shouted. "You know I was just working on the notes. They have to be on my desk."

"Now, you're being cooperative," said the blond, lifting his feet off the desk. His three associates crossed to him and began pulling out drawers and emptying their contents on the floor. The leader followed in their wake, sorting through papers. He picked up her notebook and glanced at the scrawls, then dropped it back on the floor. One of the men grabbed the dictionary and shook it violently. The single sheet drifted out and the blond man pounced on it with an expression of extreme satisfaction. His eyes flicked across the page, and smiling, he stuffed it into a pocket.

"Okay, you've got what you want," mumbled Kathy dully. "Now get out."

Smiling urbanely, the young man waved away the guards and tucked her arm beneath his. "Ah, but, Ms.

Littlebird, I'm afraid that we're going to have to take you into protective custody. The information you possess could be very dangerous to you."

"Yeah, no shit," answered Littlebird, swallowing down a mouthful of blood. "Will I get my one call?"

"But why, Ms. Littlebird? You're not under arrest."

"Oh, of course, I forgot," she muttered sarcastically.

"Besides, we wouldn't want to upset your friend, now, would we?"

Kathy thought of Sherry depending upon her to stop the deadly spraying. There was no way to warn her of the failure of their plans. Suddenly Kathy remembered that Sherry and Hutch had intended to keep working on the destruction of the flies. What if they returned to the north country without knowing of her plight? A cold fear settled into her chest, and she choked down a sob.

They'll be up there when the planes come, she thought, *and they're going to die with everything else. And there's nothing I can do to stop it.*

Chapter Sixteen

"She's not there," called Sherry as she ran back from the phone booth and slid into the seat of the idling station wagon.

"Well, that seems funny." Hutch nervously flicked his toothpick to the other side of his mouth. "I mean, we just left there an hour ago. Did you-"

"Try the office? Yep. She's not there." Sherry worried at her lower lip with her teeth, then looked up at Hutch, concern mirrored in her face. "Hutch, there's something wrong. I just sense it."

"So?"

"So let's get back to her place and check on her."

"Good idea."

Hutch pulled out of the Chevron station and into the insane traffic of Cerrillos Road. As they crawled along, Sherry's fingers beat out a nervous tattoo on the vinyl seat. At last Hutch was able to turn off the busy thoroughfare and onto the winding back streets of Santa Fe. Some of Sherry's nervousness seemed to be communicated to Hutch, for his foot began to press heavier and heavier on the gas pedal, and when they did pull into the driveway at Kathy Littlebird's, the tires squealed in protest.

They reached the door together. Hutch hammered with the knocker, then stepped back, startled, as the door swung open.

Exchanging glances, the couple burst into the

house and stood goggling at the destruction. Numbly Sherry moved through the debris, paper and furniture stuffing floating away from her feet as she stepped. Hutch picked up a book and shoved it into a bookcase.

"To borrow a phrase from our friend Dr. Fonseca," said Hutch, "I think we're playing in the big leagues." He stooped and recovered another book, then dropped it onto the one intact arm of the couch.

"Do you think she managed to get the word out?" asked Sherry.

"I doubt it." Hutch retrieved yet another volume. Sherry buried her face in her hands and began to weep. It was a hopeless, tearing sound. Even at the time of Pammy's death Hutch had never heard such a sound out of Sherry. In the silent room it was a horrible cry. Terrified, Hutch dropped the book onto the couch and rushed to her side.

In her grief she rocked from side to side, and he caught her slender body in his arms in an effort to halt the hysterical motion. Between racking sobs she began to speak, and he held her closer, trying to hear.

"I've fought so long... so hard for Pammy. Now it's all over. Soon... everything will be... dust and ashes."

"Then, to hell with it," Hutch burst out. "Let's just get out of it, live our own lives. It can't be our fight anymore. It's just gotten too big."

She lifted a tear-stained face to meet his. "But these men are evil, Hutch. How can we walk away from what they're about to do?"

"Well, shit." He jammed his hands into his pockets and paced agitatedly away from her. "Maybe their approach is the right one. We're talkin' a few thousand people if they spray in New Mexico. If they don't do something, those critters are gonna breed and maybe millions of people will die."

"I can't do anything about the millions of people across the United States, but I can try to do something about the people I've lived and worked among." Her voice was level, only a lingering trace of tears remained. Hutch's shoulders slumped when he heard the determination replace her earlier defeat.

"Sherry, honey." he half-moaned, crossing to her. "It's eleven o'clock in the morning. We've only got nineteen hours left. If all the brains in Los Alamos and Washington couldn't come up with another solution, how can we?" He caught her almost imperceptible wince when he mentioned Los Alamos, but he said nothing, even though the silence cost him a great deal of effort.

"Hutch, I will not give up!" She stalked away from him, marching back and forth across the littered room. "My child died as a result of those creatures. I can't stand by and see more children die because of evil men who can deal only in expediency. There must be some other way to destroy them, something other than the usual approach. They've tried spraying..."

Hutch flung himself onto the couch and tried to tune her out. It was a diatribe he'd heard before and he didn't have the strength for another one. He picked up the book he'd abandoned earlier, and began to flip nervously through the pages.

"Hutch!" He jumped guiltily, for the voice came from behind and over his left shoulder. "You're not listening to a word..." Her voice died away, and she suddenly hung over the back of the sofa.

"Uh... I'm sorry, honey. It's just that-" But she ignored him and jerked the book he had been staring at sightlessly from his grasp. "Sherry? Sherry? What the hell is it?" he demanded, somewhat aggrieved by her bizarre behavior.

"Hutch, look at this." She hurried around the couch and joined him on the ripped frame.

"Controlling Pests," he read aloud. "Well, I'll be damned." He half-closed the book and looked at the title. *"The Farmer's Almanack-1892.* What in the hell was Kathy doing with this?"

"You know how she is, a real trivia pack rat. But forget that. Look what it says." She reopened the book and pointed to a paragraph near the end of the page.

Hutch's eyes leaped down the page, noting the use of fly papers and various obnoxious mixtures for the destruction of flies until he reached the indicated passage.

> Flies may also be controlled by
> the playing of a deep harmonic
> tone in the vicinity of the pests.
> A harmonica or any other
> deep-voiced instrument is
> useful for this purpose.

He closed the book, using his finger to mark the place, and eyed her dubiously. "Sherry, that's just plain crazy. If the most powerful insecticides can't kill these flies, then how is a *harmonica* gonna do it?"

"Well, I know that part sounds kind of crazy, but I do know that sound waves can be deadly, and I think that's what they were trying to get at."

"Yeah, but who are we gonna ask? Fonseca?" he asked with derision. Hutch stared at Sherry's averted face and felt rage and jealousy rising within him. "Well, are we? Is that who you're gonna call after the way he deserted us?" The harshness of his tone startled him and infuriated her.

Sherry leaped to her feet and whirled on him, her face flushed with anger. "You're a fine one to judge him when not ten minutes ago you were ready to give up!"

"Yeah, but I wasn't gonna throw in with those guys from Washington," he cried, stung.

"Oh, yes, you were, at least tacitly. If it's hard for you to fight against those people's approach, then think how much harder it must be for Robert, who works with and for them."

Hutch stormed across the room to the desk and seized the phone receiver. "Okay, you call Robert," he yelled, shaking the receiver at her. "God knows you've acted like he glowed in the dark ever since you met him!"

"That's not fair," gasped Sherry.

"Oh, no? Well, let me tell you, it's been nothing but Robert this, and Robert that, and Robert will know what to do, and we have to tell Robert, for days now."

His voice had taken on a mocking singsong quality, and Sherry flinched from the tone and the inner knowledge that what he said was true. She pulled herself together and looked Hutch in the eye.

'"What you say may be true, but this isn't the time to argue about it. And this is one time that we've got to tell Robert."

"Yeah, and you want to know something? I'll bet you a thousand bucks that he won't help. He won't come."

"If *I* ask him," Sherry said coldly and deliberately, "he'll come."

Hutch silently returned the receiver to the cradle and walked across the room to stare out a window at the piñon-covered hills of Santa Fe. Sherry paused as she reached for the phone, and looked at him. His stiff back reproached her.

Trembling, she began to dial a number that had become as familiar to her as her own. Her parting shot had been cruel and dirty. She knew that. She also didn't know why she had done it. Emotional upset? Frustration? Fear? After all, she loved Hutch.

Do you love Robert Fonseca, too? whispered a small voice as the phone began to ring. Sherry squeezed her eyes shut and clutched at the phone while she willed the voice to go away.

The phone continued to ring, and she began to fear that he had not in fact returned home as she had expected him to. If not at home, then where? The lab, or-

"Hello?" He sounded old and tired, but she almost sobbed with relief at having found him.

"Robert!"

"Sherry! My God, I never thought I would hear from you again... I'm sorry about what happened earlier..."

"Robert, there's no time for that. Hutch and I may have found something that will destroy the flies and prevent the spraying. What I need to know is if it's feasible."

"Tell me," he ordered, and she quickly outlined the passage in the *Almanack*. There was a long silence, then at last he spoke, and his voice was filled with excitement.

"I think it could work. The body tissues of a fly are extremely fragile. Sound waves can set up sympathetic resonances within various materials that can cause them to shatter."

"Then, it's worth a try?"

"It's definitely worth a try. Where are you?"

"At my friend's, Kathy Littlebird's house. I'm afraid something may have happened to her, though. We came to see her early this morning and told her about Fallon's plans. Then when we came back, she was-"

"Oh, my God!"

"Robert? Are you all right?"

"Yes, but you may not be. Fallon apparently decided that you and Hutch were dangerous. He's ordered that you be rounded up and placed in protective custody until the spraying is over. If they tracked you to your friend's house, then they may track you there again. You've got to get out of there, and fast."

"But where can we go?"

Hutch seemed to sense the fear in her voice, for he drifted back from the window and stood at her side.

"Someplace where they'll never think to look for

you. The Los Alamos Inn."

"We'll be there in forty-five minutes. Registered under the name of... uh... Fallon."

He chuckled slightly. "I'll meet you there. Now, get going."

"What's up?" Hutch asked as she replaced the receiver.

"First you owe me a thousand dollars. Second, Fallon's goons are looking for us. We're going to meet Robert at the Los Alamos Inn."

As she was talking, Sherry gathered up the *Almanack* and headed for the front door. The rented station wagon was parked directly in front of the house, and Hutch didn't bother to turn around at the end of the drive. He put the car into reverse and began backing down the curving drive toward the gate.

Suddenly he saw in the rearview mirror the sleek nose of a dark sedan poke past the wood fence.

"Hang on!" he shouted, and jammed the accelerator to the floor. The big car roared backward down the drive, gravel spraying from beneath the wheels, and slammed into the front of the sedan.

Metal screeched in protest as the momentum of the station wagon shoved the other car across the narrow street and wedged the right front wheel against the far curb. Sherry, clinging to the seat back, stared out the back window.

"There's another car, but he's blocked by the first one."

"All *right!*" whooped Hutch, and threw the car into drive. As they careened away up the street, the passenger door on the wrecked sedan flew open and a suited man leaned across the roof of the car, leveling an UZI on the rapidly fleeing station wagon. There were four or five loud *whumps* as the high-speed bullets tore into the body of the car, and Sherry screamed in terror as the rear windshield frosted and starred with the impact of yet another round. Then they were around the sheltering curve in the road and speeding into the hills surrounding Santa Fe.

"We've got to get a new car," said Hutch. "We're sitting ducks in this one."

"And how are we going to do that? Go back to the rental agency?" asked Sherry somewhat acidly.

He grinned at her, and she grinned back, feeling pleased that their fight at Kathy's was apparently forgotten.

"I figure that since we've embarked on this life of crime, we may as well continue. I thought we'd steal one."

"Do you know how?"

"Yep."

"I'm not going to ask." She sighed and sank back against the seat.

Chapter Seventeen

Fonseca paid off the bellboy and, balancing the tray, kicked shut the door. Hutch lay sprawled out on one of the two double beds with his arms folded behind his head and his eyes closed, ignoring the scientist.

The clink of bottle on glass brought Sherry out of the bathroom, and she stood in the door dubiously eyeing the three glasses, ice bucket, and bottle of Johnny Walker Red.

"Do you think that's such a good idea? Maybe a clear head would help the discussion."

"As crazy as this scheme is, I'd rather be drunk to contemplate it," answered Robert, crossing to her with a glass.

"Then you don't think it can work," Sherry said, defeated, and started to turn away.

He caught her by the arm and pulled her back. "I didn't say that. In fact, the readings I did before you arrived were encouraging. I'm just saying that it's far out and we could all die trying it."

She stared at his hand, which still rested on her arm and which in fact had begun to stroke up and down the length of her sleeve. Flushing, he removed his hand and nervously ran it through his hair. She accepted the glass and moved away from him, to sit in a chair near a window.

"But if we don't try," she continued as if the interlude hadn't taken place, "thousands of people will die."

"And there's still no guarantee that the flies will be destroyed."

"Oh, yeah?" asked Hutch, sitting up and joining in the conversation for the first time.

"Yeah. They didn't do any live testing. They just took the most destructive toy in their arsenal and are banking on it to do the job."

"Great," muttered Hutch sarcastically, and fell back against the pillows.

"But back to my original question. Do you think this has a chance of working?" Sherry pushed.

Fonseca sat on the other bed and patted a pile of volumes he'd carried to the hotel. He gave them one final pat, then sighed and looked at her. "I *think* so. My readings have indicated that we need a powerful bass tone. Probably an E or a D. The problem is: What are we going to use to generate the sound? As intriguing as the thought of a harmonica might be, I'm a bit hesitant to place it as the sole defense between me and thousands of carnivorous flies."

Silence settled over the room as the trio pondered what instrument would be best suited to their purpose.

"Piano, trumpet, violin, guitar," muttered Sherry, "No, none of those would work." She threw up her hands in disgust and sank back in the chair.

"A synthesizer would be perfect," remarked Fonseca. "Unfortunately we don't have one."

"Also, how would we get it up there," added Hutch. "The organ!" cried Sherry, slipping from her chair and racing to Hutch's bed.

"Huh?"

"You know! The old organ in the church in Trinidad." She bounced vigorously on the mattress, causing Hutch to grab for the edge of the bed.

He struggled to a sitting position and seized her by the waist, forcing her to stop her nervous jumping.

"Hold it. That organ is old, and it barely worked the day you tried it."

"But it *did* work, and we can make it work again."

"You know anything about organs?" argued Hutch.

"Well, I can learn!"

"In... ah"- he looked at his watch - "sixteen hours?"

Sherry militantly thrust out her chin and opened her mouth to speak.

"Before this deteriorates any further, may I say something?" broke in Fonseca.

"What?" the couple demanded together.

"Oddly enough I *do* know something about organs. Not a lot, but enough to get sound out of it for the minute or two we would need." Dumbfounded, Sherry and Hutch stared at him. Fonseca shrugged sheepishly. "What can I say? When I was a kid I thought I wanted to be a selfless physician serving the poor. Schweitzer was my idol, and since he was an organist, I hung around the church organ and read a few books."

"Great. So we go up in the mountains, turn on the organ, and the flies say, 'You die'," grumbled Hutch.

"A good point. Obviously we're going to have to augment the sound."

Hutch swung off the bed and stared at his companions. "Are we really going through with this?" he asked, his eyes pinning each one.

Sherry met his gaze and nodded without hesitation. A faint shudder seemed to shake Fonseca's stocky frame, then a few seconds later, he too nodded.

"Okay, then we need amps, a generator, and a microphone pickup."

"Where do we get those?"

"Not we, me. You're known around here, Doc, so I'll be the one to buy the junk. Only thing, though, Sherry and I don't have the money. You're gonna have to kick in."

"Of course." The scientist pulled out his checkbook and wrote out a draft. "Will that do?"

Hutch stared at the amount for several minutes, then swallowed heavily and nodded. "I'll hit the bank on my way to White Rock, then if they don't have what we need, I'll head on down to Santa Fe."

"Is that safe?" asked Sherry with a frown.

"Shit, yeah, honey. They'll never expect us to come *back*." He started for the door, then paused and added, "I'll rent a four-wheel-drive truck too. God knows we're gonna need it to haul all this crap up there."

Sherry slipped off the bed and ran to his side. Feverishly she pressed her lips against his and held him tightly against her. "Hutch, be careful. Please be careful."

For a moment he buried his face in the fragrance of her long hair, then he set her aside with a grin. "Hell, yes, I'll be careful; it's you two I'm worried about. Don't go opening the door to any of those goons while I'm gone."

"As if we would be so stupid," responded Sherry, forcing a laugh and punching him lightly on the chest.

"Well, okay. I'll see you guys later." Hutch looked from one to the other with a strained expression. The door shut firmly behind him.

Sherry retrieved her drink and downed it in one gulp. "He knows," she stated flatly.

"What? That I love you? If he's worried about that, he's going to be worried for the rest of his life. A man hasn't been born who could resist you, Sherry," he concluded quietly.

"That's silly. Don't talk that way." She paced to the table and splashed more Scotch into her glass.

"It's silly that I love you?"

"Yes... I mean, no... I, I don't know." She gulped at the drink and noticed that her hand was trembling. Angrily she wrapped both hands about the glass.

"Shall I show you that I'm far from being silly?"

She jerked her head up, her eyes searching for his. They were very golden, almost catlike, and she began to feel like some small animal who knows it is prey. Suddenly she banged her glass down onto the tabletop and threw back her hair.

"I've never been hunted before, and I don't like men who don't deal straight from the shoulder with me."

He stared down at his sleeve and brushed a piece of lint from the jacket. "Well," he said with a chagrined smile, "another of my practiced and time-honored acts collapses before my remarkable lady."

Sherry relaxed from her rigid stance and joined him on the edge of the bed. "Is this how you always put on the moves?"

"Yes."

"No wonder you're not married."

"Is it that offensive?" he asked, drawing back from her.

"That's not what I meant. Any woman who would weaken and succumb to an act like that isn't woman enough for you, and I think underneath it all you know that and feel safe."

"Ever considered a career in psychology?" he asked lightly. He paused, then turned to look at her. "I'm sorry. It was rude and demeaning to treat you that way. Will you forgive me?"

She studied him, noting the sincerity in his deep voice and the contrite expression on his round face. Her eyes lingered on his face, and she mentally traced the line of his upswept brows, the full underlip, the squarish jaw. Softer, rounder, it was very different from Hutch's rugged features, which looked as if they had been hewn with an ax, but it was a handsome face and one she had come to love.

She pondered the emotion that she had discovered within herself, turning it over and over before her mind's eye. At last, reluctantly she acknowledged it to be real, and she realized that she had to deal with her love for both these men.

Fonseca had risen and crossed to the table to pour another drink. He saluted her with his glass and asked flippantly, "Well, shall we discuss impressionistic painting? How about the state of the fashion industry?" Sherry rose slowly to her feet and walked to him, never taking her eyes from his. She stopped within inches of him and languidly ran her hand up the front of his chest. The material rasped gently under her work-worn fingertips. A small voice was yammering somewhere in the back of her mind that this was crazy, and she had to think things through.

She squelched it firmly, deciding that if she survived the next day, *then* she would think things through.

Fonseca's glass fell from suddenly nerveless fingers. The Scotch soaked unnoticed into the beige carpet as his arms slipped about her. His mouth came down on hers, possessing and far more demanding than the kiss they had shared only two nights ago.

Fire washed through her, her knees buckled, and she sagged against him. He swept her up and carried her to the bed, but he stopped short and set her on her feet once more. Surprised, she opened her eyes and looked questioningly at him. He smiled reassuringly, and slowly, almost reverently, began to undress her.

She reached for the buttons on his shirt, but he stopped her with a quick shake of his head. "No, not today," he whispered against her ear. "Today I serve you for your pleasure only." Between words his tongue caressed the sensitive earlobe so that a faint gasp was her only answer. Soon she stood nude before him, and his hands swept down her body. He cupped her high, firm breasts, then his fingers moved on, pausing to linger on the prominent ribs of her whip-lean body, until at last he spanned her narrow waist with his hands and lifted her onto the bed.

A few moments later he had stripped and joined her. She arched toward him, but he held her off and proceeded to play across her body, his long slender fingers teasing and titillating. He seemed to know instinctively which were her most sensitive points, and her pleasure and passion spiraled upward until she almost screamed for release.

Grinning devilishly, he began to kiss his way up her body. When he reached her lips, he gently lowered his body onto her sweat-slick skin, and she moaned her need.

Their joining was explosive, and her world narrowed to a circle of burning sensation. Spent at last, they lay quietly in each other's arms. Forgotten were the flies, the impending spraying, and Hutch.

They showered together, dressed, and returned to sit across the room from each other. Sherry gazed silently out the window while Fonseca pretended to read. They didn't speak again until Hutch returned, and then they were all too busy for words.

The headlights of the powerful four-wheel-drive truck stabbed out across the dark piñon-clad hills as the vehicle rounded yet another curve. Hutch checked in the rearview mirror to make sure that the enormous twenty-five-kilowatt generator on its separate trailer mount was staying with them. All they would need would be to have the trailer hitch break when they were within an hour of their destination, he thought, and his teeth clamped down on the rapidly disintegrating toothpick.

Sherry sat next to him on the wide seat of the truck. Occasionally the sway of the cab would throw her against him and her shoulder would brush his. Normally such an occurrence would have comforted him, but this night Sherry seemed more a statue than a live woman.

Her body was stiff and unyielding, and her blue eyes stared almost unblinking out the front window. Superstitiously Hutch felt that she was seeing something beyond the night and the highway, but he was too scared to ask what.

On the other side of Sherry, Fonseca leaned against the door, and he appeared to be sleeping. He had traded his usual suit coat for a sturdy leather jacket, and his arms were folded tightly across the breast of the coat.

So he's not sleeping, thought Hutch when he noticed the taut muscles in the other man's arms. *Guess that means he's as scared as I am. Kinda wish he were asleep, he concluded dolefully and looked back to the road.*

Hutch had driven the northern mountains for years, and it was eerie to have traveled for nearly two hours without meeting a single car. *Must mean everybody's dead, or too terrified to leave home,* he grunted to himself. *Wish I were safe in a cave somewhere. That way...*

His mental grumblings were interrupted by a blaze of headlights approaching. Suddenly a powerful searchlight shot out from the roof of the other car and seared the cab of the truck. Sherry gave a cry of alarm and Hutch threw one arm over his face, trying to regain his sight. As they flashed past the brilliantly lit automobile, Sherry pointed through the driver's window. Squinting, Hutch was able to distinguish the insignia of the New Mexico state police.

"Oh, fuck!" spat Hutch.

"Just keep going," Sherry ordered. "Maybe they won't bother us."

"An unlikely chance, I think," Fonseca said as he twisted about in the seat to gaze out the back window. "They're turning around and coming after us.

The hypnotic *flash, flash, flash* of the red light beat through the cab. Hutch chewed at the toothpick, his face a mask of indecision.

"Shit, it's no use, I'll have to pull over. I can't

outrun them with that trailer up behind."

Hutch lifted his foot from the accelerator and eased onto the shoulder. The truck skidded a bit in the soft dirt on the side of the road, and Fonseca drew in a sharp breath.

"Be careful! There's a long drop on this side and all we'd need is to go over the cliff."

The truck rolled to a stop, and Hutch rolled down the window and looked back at the now-motionless police car. A familiar massive figure was climbing from the driver's side.

"Christ! It's Padilla, and he's alone."

"Do you suppose they're looking for us?" asked Sherry.

"I think we can bet on it," broke in Fonseca.

"Hutch," Sherry pleaded, "we can't be stopped. Not when we're so close." The blond rancher stared at her for several seconds and ran a hand nervously over his face. His lips tightened with determination, and he nodded.

"Quick, Sherry, under the seat." Fonseca looked puzzled, but the woman understood and quickly obeyed. She slithered onto the floor of the cab and groped beneath the seat. A moment later she emerged triumphant with a holstered Smith & Wesson .44 Magnum.

Fonseca stared in horror at the six-and-a-half-inch barrel as Hutch pulled the weapon from its leather casing. "You... you're carrying that?" babbled the scientist.

"Damn right," responded Hutch as he spun the chamber and checked the load.

"But you had it concealed, and that's illegal!"

"Doc, not to be rude or anything, but there's a lot more at stake here than our debating gun control. Padilla is a badass, and if he's workin' for the feds, I wouldn't put it past him to try and kill us. Remember, those goons shot at Sherry and me yesterday."

Fonseca opened his mouth to speak, but the crunch of boot heels was audible in the sand. Hutch swiftly buckled the belt and holster about his waist and covered the gun with his coat. Armed and ready, he pushed open the door and stepped out to meet the Mexican cop.

"I thought I recognized you, hombre." Padilla grinned. "What you all doing? Out for a little ride?" He leered.

"Last time I looked there was no law against it," drawled Hutch.

"Oh, *sí*, for law-abiding citizens, but not for dangerous subversives like the three of you."

Hutch whistled with admiration. "Say, where did you learn a big word like that, Padilla? Musta been from some of those thugs in black suits, huh?"

The burly captain's face twisted into an expression of hatred as he stared up at the lean man before him. "Just keep talking, Engels. Every word is adding years to your sentence."

"Oh, so now you're the judge and jury too, is that it?"

"Turn around and spread 'em! You two get out of the truck!"

"Captain, please," cried Sherry as she scrambled from the high cab. "You've got to let us go on. We have a way to destroy the flies and save the people!"

"Like hell," he said derisively.

"Listen to her," called Fonseca as he made his way around the front of the vehicle to join his friends. "I'm the scientist who created the flies and I tell you this can work."

"I don't care if you're the Pope. All I know is the promotion I'm looking at if I bring you scum in. So I'm bringing you in. Besides, they warned us that you might try to sell some load of bull about them killin' all the people."

"You stupid pig!" yelled Hutch, his control breaking. "They *are* gonna kill the people. We sat there and listened to them discuss it."

Padilla's lips drew back in a snarl. "You fucking gringo. I hated you the minute I laid eyes on you, and now you gonna die! Bringin' in two of you will be enough."

Sherry screamed and darted forward, only to be brought up short by Fonseca's powerful arms. For Hutch time seemed to distend. He saw Padilla's beefy hand go for the Colt Python that hung at his hip. Throwing back the tail of his coat, Hutch grabbed the butt of his pistol and brought it up.

Too late, he thought regretfully as he saw a flash reflect off the chrome-plated barrel of Padilla's enormous gun.

He squeezed off one shot, and his hand rose with the recoil from the .44. There would be no time for another, and he waited for the bullet from Padilla's Python to tear through his chest.

It didn't come. Instead, red blossomed across the front of the policeman's brown shirt, and he crumpled backward as if hit by a mighty fist. Both hands flew into the air, and the Colt roared harmlessly at the sky.

Sherry tore from Fonseca's grasp and ran to Hutch's side. His left arm went automatically around her as he shoved the Magnum into its holster.

"What do we do now?" asked Fonseca with a calmness that bordered on hysteria.

"Put him in the car and send it over the cliff," grunted Hutch.

"Hutch," whispered Sherry, "what if-"

"They link it to me?" She nodded. "I don't think that's too likely." He bent and recovered his shell casing. "I've got my brass, and God knows Padilla had plenty of enemies."

He stepped to the truck and took out his work gloves. Pulling them on, he seized the Spaniard beneath the armpits and dragged him to the patrol car. Fonseca moved to Sherry as she watched Hutch wrestle the massive body into the car.

"Sherry, I don't think he'll be caught. Remember things are in a state of emergency. I'm certain there must have been civil breakdown. Besides," he added with a wan smile, "if we succeed, we'll be heroes, and I doubt the government wants to draw any more attention to this situation than they have to."

"Please God you're right," she murmured as Hutch removed the brake and sent the car plunging over the lip of the canyon. The explosion lit the night and for an instant etched her face in flame. "But, oh, Robert, maybe we're no better than the people we oppose: look what we've done in the name of justice."

He stood silent as she walked to meet Hutch, for there was no answer.

Chapter Eighteen

"We made it," Sherry whispered, and buried her face in her hands.

"What time is it?" asked Hutch as he stroked her hair soothingly.

"Nine thirty two," Fonseca answered as he read the flashing numerals.

"Such precision," Sherry said with a shaky laugh.

"Of course, I'm a scientist. Well, shall we get to it?"

They all piled from the cab of the truck and Hutch unhooked the trailer hitch. Running back to the truck, he pulled the bed clear of the generator. He and Fonseca then climbed into the bed and began unloading the giant concert amplifiers. They were working with only the headlights of the truck for illumination, and the near-dark conditions slowed their progress. At one point one of the cabinets caught on the metal and then broke loose with a rending shriek. Sherry, carrying wire from the truck to the church, froze in her tracks and stared nervously off toward the garbage dump.

"Don't worry," Fonseca called softly. "I doubt they'll fly at night unless it's an extreme emergency."

"Hope so," she muttered, and continued on her way.

Sweating and straining, the two men wrestled the amps into position. Fonseca paused to make several calculations. With a groan he indicated to Hutch that one of the cabinets had to be adjusted slightly to the left.

"It's critical that we send as much of the sound as possible directly into the nest. What I'm trying to set up is almost a cross-fire effect," he explained.

"Sounds good to me," said Hutch as he wiped at his face. Sherry choked and giggled, and Fonseca tried to hide a smile. "What's so funny?" asked Hutch somewhat belligerently.

"An unintended pun that really wasn't all that funny."

"Guess it just shows how tired and frightened we all are," added Sherry, and the smiles faded. Silently they returned to work.

Once the amplifiers were in position, Hutch gestured to Fonseca. "Sherry and I can handle the wiring to the generator, so you better get in and go to work on that organ. All we'd need is to go to all this work and then have it croak and snivel on us tomorrow."

Fonseca nodded briskly and vanished into the black interior of the ruined church, carrying one of the two powerful flashlights that Hutch had purchased. Sherry joined Hutch and they began to make the connections to the generator.

During the next two hours the night was filled with strange groaning noises that slowly began to resemble music. After the couple completed the work on the generator, they headed back to the church, ready to make the final connection of the microphone pickup. Suddenly the darkness sang as a brief phrase of Bach lilted through the empty windows of the looming building.

Sherry found herself shivering at the eeriness of the ghostly sound. She wrapped her arms about herself and fought down a rising, choking panic. Hutch looked back at her inquiringly, and clenching her teeth, she forced herself to walk into the shadowed interior of the church. As she crept down the aisle toward the organ, figures flickered in a macabre dance across the walls.

Robert rose stiffly to meet them. His face was streaked with dust and cobwebs adorned his jacket. One was draped, unnoticed, in his hair, and Sherry reached out and gently brushed it away. Fonseca caught her hand and held it tightly.

"Time?" breathed Hutch softly, and the whisper went hissing about the gloomy nave.

"Three ten."

"Maybe we should get in position."

Fonseca reluctantly nodded, but none of them moved. Instead they stood staring desperately at one another. Sherry gave a little sob and slipped her arms around the scientist's stocky form. For a long moment he pressed her against him, memorizing the feel of her body, the fragrance of her hair. At last she stepped back, and he and Hutch gripped each other strongly by the forearms.

Hutch swept up his flashlight, and he and Sherry retreated from the church. Both their golden heads seemed to be shimmering in the faint light, and Fonseca pressed a hand against his chest, trying to will away the knot of pain that had settled there.

Their light vanished, and Fonseca turned to face the altar. Slowly he crossed himself. It was an act he had not made for many years. His back found the organ, and he slid down the side of the instrument to the floor to wait. It would be a distant dawn.

At the door of the church Sherry and Hutch embraced. Breaking apart, they crossed to the truck, and reaching into the cab, Hutch pulled out a camera and binoculars. Sherry accepted them and with a final nod walked to her position behind and to the left of the amplifiers.

Hutch fought down the need to rush after her and hold on to her. He hunched his shoulders and viciously jerked out the radio phone Fonseca had obtained for them just before their departure from Los Alamos. It was already set to the Kirtland frequency, and it had fallen to Hutch to radio if their plan succeeded. He only hoped they would listen.

Slinging the radio over one shoulder, he moved to his place several hundred feet to the right of Sherry. Even as he tested the equipment, his attention was on the woman. He wondered if she were sleeping, or if she too were plagued with fears.

Hutch remembered how Sherry had held Fonseca, and he squeezed his eyes shut against the sting of tears. He wanted to hate Robert Fonseca, but he couldn't. They had become like brothers, but brothers who loved the same woman.

If we all survive this, who will she go with? And if she chooses him, how can I stand it? So his thoughts ran as he waited for daybreak.

Sherry lay on her back, staring sightlessly at the star-strewn sky. She didn't think of the two men waiting near her. Rather she watched as her beautiful girl-child galloped across high mountain meadows with her golden braids flying. And she dreamed of revenge.

Gold-and-pink streamers shot up in the west as the sun began to clear the high peaks surrounding Trinidad. Sherry stood tensely gazing through the binoculars toward the dump. A light breeze sprang up, fluttering her hair behind her, and borne on the wind was the throbbing drone of the flies.

Beyond the distant ridge a black cloud began to rise. Sherry, with the powerful field glasses, could distinguish individuals in the swarm. She swung the binoculars in a quick arc and picked out at least fifteen of the mammoth flies.

For Hutch, squatting on the ground by the radio, it looked as if some hideous, evil entity was climbing over the rocky incline. It seemed to hang poised and swaying in the air, then it plunged over the edge.

"Now!" screamed out Sherry.

Inside the church Fonseca heard her faint call. He shifted on the organ bench and forcefully depressed one of the powerful bass pedals. The deep droning note was captured by the amplifiers and pulsed out toward the advancing flies.

Seconds ticked away. Sherry's hands became slippery with sweat as she gripped the binoculars and waited. Nothing. Nothing. Nothing. Her body seemed to vibrate from the tone and the diesel thrumming of the generator. The pressure mounted, and she twisted her head to one side and gasped for air.

And still the flies advanced. Suddenly the amplifiers cut out, leaving only the muffled drone of the organ from within the church. Hutch belly-crawled frantically toward his large amplifier and wriggled the lead. It had no effect. He looked desperately from the still placidly chugging generator to the stubbornly silent amplifiers.

"Hutch! For the love of God!" sobbed Sherry over the deadly buzz of the advancing flies. "Do something!"

Leaping to his feet, the man raced for the generator. Sweat stung his eyes and his breath burned in his chest as he sprinted across the grass.

He reached the generator and began reattaching the leads. A hideous weight settled between his shoulder blades, and at the same moment Sherry gave a wail of terror and warning. Crouching, Hutch spun, doubled his fist, and slugged with all his might at the giant fly that hovered above him. His blow shattered the fragile exoskeleton, and his hand sunk deep into the spongy body. He didn't wait to see where the monster fell, but just turned back to the generator.

He grasped the last plug as a clot of flies settled onto his hands. He screamed in agony, but he forced himself to thrust the lead home. The blast of sound from the amplifiers staggered him, and he fell to the ground, rolling to dislodge the sucking, feeding horror.

Sherry, who had buried her face in her arms, waiting for death, lifted her head when the sound began again. -

Too late, she thought wildly, for the insects were almost upon her.

Then with a horrible mushy, popping sound they began to explode. Cheering like a madwoman, Sherry dropped the glasses and seized her camera. She snapped frame after frame, imprinting forever the proof of the creature's destruction.

With almost morbid fascination she followed one of the enormous flies into the net of sound. Frame: It beat grotesquely through the clear air with its transparent wings producing its hideous buzz. Frame: The smooth rhythm of its wing sweeps flattened. Frame: Almost in slow motion its bloated body burst outward. Bits of glistening black tissue rained to the ground followed by a great gout of internal fluids.

The generator chugged heavily, the massive bass note seeming to increase in sound and potency, but the illusion was the result of the diminishing buzz of the great swarm, the dreaded sound fading as the organ tone reached the dump and the flies died in the midst of their garbage feasting.

Chapter Nineteen

The throbbing bass reached its lowest pitch. Suddenly bits of adobe began to patter down upon Sherry. Glancing up, she saw the forty-foot wall of the church shaking and crumbling beneath the force of the tone.

As she raced for the door of the building, beams and struts from the old bell towers crashed about her. One struck her a glancing blow across the head, but she kept her feet and continued to run.

She was brought to the ground by a crushing impact. Fighting like a wildcat, she twisted about in Hutch's arms and beat on him with the camera. He forced the camera from her hand and thrust it into one pocket. Hutch struggled to his feet and pulled her after him. The front of the church collapsed, bringing with it the pipes for the organ. The bass note ceased abruptly and Sherry's screams could now be heard over the generator.

"Robert! Robert! Robert!" Her cries faded into sobs as the remaining three walls fell in on themselves. "We've got to get to him! Help him! Hutch, please," she cried hysterically.

Hutch gripped her by the wrists and shook her. "Sherry, it's no use. No one could have survived that."

"But we've got to try!"

"Sherry! The planes are coming! We've got to radio!"

"Then do it!" she screamed, and broke free from his hold. He bolted after her, then froze with indecision between the fleeing woman and the beckoning radio. With an oath he ran to the radio phone and switched it on.

Her nails were soon cut and bleeding as she scrabbled and dug through the rubble. She burrowed among fallen rafters, inching her way toward what had once been the front of the church. Her boot dislodged a beam, and dirt rained down on her. Choking, she spat the dust from her mouth and called, "Robert?"

There was a faint moan to her right. Desperately she fought her way through the debris until her hand touched cloth.

He was pinned by one of the massive beams that had supported the roof. His eyes were closed and he breathed in shallow moaning breaths. Each time he exhaled, a tiny rivulet of blood trickled from his mouth.

With the pragmatism born of ranch life, Sherry knew that he was dying. Inching past his body, she took his head in her lap and gently stroked his hair. His topaz eyes fluttered open and he looked at her.

She bent and kissed him softly on the forehead. "Robert," she whispered, "I love you."

He smiled sweetly up at her, then his eyes filmed and he was gone.

"Come in, come in, Kirtland. This is Hutch Engels!"

"We read you, Engels, and what in the hell are you doing on this band?"

"Call off the planes!"

"How did you-"

"It's over! The flies are destroyed. You've got to stop that spraying!"

"Who *are* you?"

"I *told* you," screamed Hutch, almost sobbing with

frustration. "Tell Fallon. He's got to be around there someplace, and he'll know who I am."

"This is Harold Fallon, Mr. Engels. What have you got to say?"

"I'm sitting up at Trinidad with mashed fly bodies all around me, and if you don't stop those planes, Sherry and I, not to mention everybody else, are going to die."

"How do I know you're telling the truth?"

"We've got pictures, and you have my word."

"That's not good enough."

From the south Hutch began to hear the whine of F-15 engines. He beat on the ground in desperation. Over the radio he heard another voice in the background.

"We could always pull one plane out of formation and send it over to investigate."

"Yes, yes!" Hutch screamed. "Do it!"

"Are you certain, General?"

"Five minutes isn't going to make that much difference, Mr. Fallon, and I'm all in favor of determining if this spraying is unnecessary."

"Very well, then."

Hutch released a breath that he hadn't been aware he'd been holding. Shading his eyes, he looked to the south at the now visible formation of planes. Seconds later one broke off from the rest, and dived toward him.

As the plane howled in, Hutch leaped to his feet and frantically waved both arms over his head. The F-15 nosed up, banked, and came in for another look.

Hutch knelt once more by the radio and grabbed the receiver. "Did he see? Did he see?"

"Yes, Mr. Engels, the pilot has given confirmation. Congratulations, sir, it isn't often that we back down from a decision."

The jet had reached its fellows, and the entire formation turned and headed back south toward the base. Hutch flipped off the radio and sat, drained, on the dry summer grass.

A touch on the shoulder pulled him from his stunned reverie. Sherry stood over him. Her hair was matted and her face and clothing were brown with dirt.

"I stopped them," he said simply.

"I knew you could."

"The doc?"

"Gone."

She settled next to him and rested her head on his shoulder.

Absently he stroked her hair. "Sherry," he began. "I was wondering-"

"No." She placed a finger against his lips. "Let's not play 'what if.' I love you, Hutch. We'll leave it at that."

He nodded, and they sat silently for a long while. "The universe is very cruel, Hutch," Sherry said at last. "It casts us in our roles, and we play out its game."

"I beg pardon?"

"Oh, sorry. Several weeks ago I felt like I had become a Fury in some Greek tragedy. Now I'm certain I was right. We all had our parts. Robert, the great man brought low because of hubris; you, the warrior; and Pammy..." She paused and stared off across the meadow. "Pammy provided the victim, the motivation for the play to begin."

"I don't know about all that stuff, honey. All I know is that we won, and we're alive, and we've got a life to plan for."

"Yes, it's time we buried our dead."

She rose and extended a hand to Hutch. He took it, and together they walked toward the truck. At the cab she stopped and looked back toward the ruined church. Her gaze shifted, and she stared out across the wildflower-dotted meadow.

In her mind's eye a bright-eyed child rode gaily across the field to be met by a stocky, golden-eyed man who lifted her from her white pony and held her strongly in his arms.

Sherry smiled through her tears and lifted her hand in farewell.

About the Author

Mark Kendall was born in Capetown, South Africa in 1942. He is a cultural anthropologist, currently living in Santa Fe, New Mexico. He is a crack shot, and an expert horseman who flew medical supplies to Biafra during the Nigerian Civil War.